THE TITAN PROTOTYPE

A NOVEL BY MICHAEL COLE

THE TITAN PROTOTYPE

Copyright © 2023 MICHAEL COLE
Copyright © 2023 by Severed Press

WWW.SEVEREDPRESS.COM

All rights reserved. No part of this book may be reproduced or transmitted in any form or by any electronic or mechanical means, including photocopying, recording or by any information and retrieval system, without the written permission of the publisher and author, except where permitted by law.
This novel is a work of fiction. Names, characters, places and incidents are the product of the author's imagination, or are used fictitiously. Any resemblance to actual events, locales or persons,
living or dead, is purely coincidental.

ISBN: 978-1-923165-89-2

All rights reserved.

CHAPTER 1

“Ah, ha! I bet you guys haven’t seen this one before.”

A chorus of groans filled the interior of the SH-60 Seahawk helicopter. Though retired from active service, it did not mean the machine did not do the bidding of the U.S. Government. Only this time, they had to pay for more than its manufacture and repair.

While his private strike team endured the showboating of Jarman and his magic tricks, Captain Andrew Serrano watched the blackness of the world on the other side of that window. It was the usual way things progressed. Jarman ‘entertained’ the team with his usual antics. All the while, Serrano gazed out the window.

Flying over the Indian Ocean at two in the morning, there was not much to see. Just blackness. In a sense, that was better. The darkness consuming this side of the planet enabled the former Army captain to visualize his assignment. He knew the kind of men their target surrounded himself with. All bad guys, all of whom with murderous history—exactly the kind of company their objective attracted. Armed conflict was inevitable.

Serrano was no stranger to taking life, nor to close calls. Experience forged wisdom.

The men went back and forth, with Jarman showing off his latest grand illusions that he learned on YouTube in his spare time. Most of the time, it was some kind of ‘pick a card’ type of routine. Today, it had something to do with making an object seemingly disappear.

“They’re all the same, ya Houdini wannabe,” Little protested.

"If you were really good, you'd change this guy's name to something a little more... fitting," Kresmery said.

That got a laugh from the team, and a groan from Little. The biggest member of the group, his last name led to the repeat of the same joke, which never got old. Not even for Seranno, though he would never admit it.

Jarman, a marine of eight years experience—now a private contractor with six, all under Serrano's employment—scratched his thin red beard while he waited for an opportunity to resume showing off. He sat in his seat, close to the door gunner, Cam. Cam's real name was Mac, which everyone remarked was too cliché for this line of work thanks to Hollywood. He fit the part though, being the stern-faced silent type. Like Seranno, he was in business mode. He was not here for laughs. He was here to kick ass and pump lead.

"Now pay attention."

"Do we have to?" Weston, the demolitions expert, asked.

"As long as you're stuck in this bird with me, you may as well enjoy the entertainment," Jarman said. "Beats looking at pictures of your kids all day."

Weston folded up his little pocketbook. In it were kid photos of his two young boys, both of whom were now adults.

"Be nice," Little said, eager to redirect the team from the subject of his last name. "Bomb voyage here got a birthday present from his oldest. Surprised he isn't showing it off right now."

"Yeah, I saw the little peashooter he got ya," Jarman said. "Congrats, he got you a snub nose, Smith. Why you decided to bring that along while you have cooler, *bigger* guns to play with is beyond me. Now, for the last time..."

"No such thing as a gun too small," Weston said.

Jarman pursed his lips, fed up with the constant interruptions. "Now, for my next trick…"

"You will shut the fuck up?" Kresmery asked. Another laugh from the group followed.

Holding up his middle finger, Jarman continued. "I got this pin…"

Now he had the team's attention, including Cam's. All of them beheld the sight of the grenade pin in Jarman's right hand, and the live grenade in his left. It was clenched in his fist, keeping the lever in the proper place.

"Dude!" Weston said, pointing a finger. "If you drop that, I'll be sure to shoot you before it blows us, just so I can have the satisfaction."

Jarman sniggered. "Would you relax for even half a second? I'm a pro—oh, fuck!" He leaned forward, fixing his grip on the grenade after accidentally bumping his elbow against the bulkhead.

All eyes widened.

"For a second there, I thought our target was going to perform the magic trick," Little said. "Blow us out of the sky without even firing a shot."

"Shut up now," Jarman said. "Now, here's the pin. Now, watch the pin. It's here. It's there." He moved his hand in weird motions as if he was a wizard about to cast a spell on his teammates. In a swift motion, he pretended to brush his hair. When his hand came back into view, all of a sudden, the key was gone.

The team watched intently, not out of interest for his trick, but in suspense of whether it would actually end up back in the grenade.

"Oh! Where could it be?" Jarman said. "Could it be here?" He sat up and checked his seat. No key. He leaned forward, ensuring he did not tuck it in his hair. "Uh-oh! Where do you think it went?"

"Don't know, but I know where *you'll* go if you don't find it right quick," Weston said. He nodded at the fuselage door. Cam nodded, more than happy to do the deed.

Smiling, Jarman leaned to the mercenary seated next to him. Blake stiffened, less than enthusiastic to see Jarman reaching for his back pocket.

"Not sure about you, but I'm not into that sort of thing," he said. "We all know how you marines like it in the ass, but the rest of us…"

"Just hang on," Jarman said. He shifted his arm for Blake's left ear. "Ah-HA!... wait…"

He glanced around, his unnerved expression getting everyone's heart racing. The idiot wasn't faking it.

He stood up, now holding the grenade in both hands to be absolutely sure he didn't screw up any further.

Finally, Serrano stepped in. "Right there, dumbass." He pointed at the jarhead's own back pocket. Jarman looked down at himself, breathing a sigh of relief after seeing the pin's ring barely protruding from his back pocket. It was such dumb luck that it landed there, it may as well have been a magic trick.

Grinning nervously, he placed the pin back where it belonged. "Whoops. Must've lost my grip on that while I was trying to…"

"That's enough with the bullshit, Jarman," Serrano said.

The embarrassed jarhead gave a toothy smile and took his seat. "It's magic. It's a skill, Captain."

"Not one you possess," Serrano said. "Now listen up. We're getting close to the drop-off point. As long as *Gandalf* here doesn't curse us with any more antics, we should have this done and be home by breakfast. That being said, don't underestimate our target."

"Ah, Dr. Nore, the animal doctor. Worried about a lab geek, Cap?"

Serrano looked to the back of the compartment where Rymer, a former Army corporal, sat. A good marksman and soldier, but a little cocky. With that attitude along with the face tattoos, Serrano would have pegged him for some college dropout who got caught up in a street gang had it not been for his military record. At twenty-eight years old and with too many confirmed kills to count, Rymer suffered from an invincibility complex. On more than one occasion, Serrano had to remind him of the risk of underestimating an enemy.

"As a matter of fact, yes," Serrano said. "As you generously reminded us, Dr. Hank Nore is our target. He has been involved with over a dozen Top Secret projects with the U.S. government. Obviously, the 'top secret' part prevents us from knowing exactly what the nature of those projects were, but if we go with his specialty, it probably has something to do with chemical weapons and genetic engineering."

"What's he doing all the way out here?" Little asked.

"Whatever it is, it's not in service of our client," Serrano said. "What we do know is Dr. Nore is in cahoots with a Russian arms dealer named Baranov. It's safe to say he's working on new weapons, likely chemical in nature, which may be used against the U.S. and its allies. Considering current events, our client is not very enthused about their former contractor working with someone whom they consider an enemy.

"He's on a cargo ship called the *Griffin*, owned by that arms dealer I mentioned. We believe that ship has been used for shipping weapons into Africa and southeast Asia. We know Dr. Nore is currently on that ship, as well as whatever it is he is working on. Its exact destination is unknown, nor is it relevant. Not to us, at least. Our job is to capture Dr. Nore and bring him stateside. In addition, they want photos of whatever it is that ship might be carrying."

Serrano looked at Jarman. "Hope you're better with a camera than you are your so-called magic tricks."

The jarhead raised his hands and made a rectangle with his thumbs and index finger, putting the Captain in frame. "Click, click."

"Ya forgot to smile, Captain," Rymer said.

Serrano considered a crass response, instead continuing with the rest of the briefing. "Once we have Nore and the photos, our orders are to destroy all of Nore's research that is on that ship. Weston, your job is to carry the incendiary explosives. Intel suspects a large number of armed crewmen aboard the vessel. If shit hits the fan, obtaining Dr. Nore is our primary objective. That said, our client wants the research destroyed so Baranov's half-assed scientists can't try and duplicate it."

"How many hostiles?" Weston asked.

"More than your little six-shooter can handle," Jarman said.

"At least sixty," Serrano said. "Considering the man Dr. Nore is working with, these men were all hand-picked. These are not everyday seamen trying to make a living. Nor are they conscripted civilians doing their government's bidding. Each one of these guys has the kind of rap sheet you'd expect Rymer to have when you look at his face."

The Corporal grinned, playing along while a couple of his teammates sniggered at his expense.

"What if the not-so-good doctor doesn't want to be taken alive?" Weston asked.

Serrano rested his hand on his rifle. The XM7 had quickly become a new favorite of his. It had good stopping power, little recoil, and best of all, accurate aim. Serrano never had an issue putting a round through someone's eye with this weapon.

Or through their kneecaps, if the situation called for it.

"We'll persuade him."

The team liked that answer.

"Five minutes from the drop-off point," Lasso, the chopper pilot, announced. Like Cam, he was the type who only spoke when necessary.

"These guys get full shares?" Jarman asked, gesturing at the cockpit and over at Cam.

"Correct," Serrano replied.

Jarman stuck his tongue out. "Lucky pricks. Get to sit back while we do all the work."

"Hey, we could just leave your ass on that boat," Cam said.

"Don't tempt us," Weston said.

"Too late," Little added.

Smirking, Jarman looked at his Captain, ready to involve him in the banter. Instead, he kept his lips zipped. Serrano was looking out the window again, using the blackness to shape his mindset. The time for jokes and games had passed. He was on business mode.

In a few minutes, they would punch that clock.

CHAPTER 2

Immediately upon arrival, Lasso brought the chopper to within a few feet of the water. The Zodiac, carried underneath the bird by a cargo hook, touched the water. Lasso held position while the team assembled at the fuselage door.

Serrano deployed a set of fast ropes and snapped his fingers at his team.

"Let's go, ladies. Jarman, you're first. Get in there."

Jarman, as instructed, was first to board the inflatable. Next was Weston, who gave an exaggerated groan after taking a seat beside him. Blake was at the helm, while Kresmery and Little sat in the back. Both professional snipers, they were looking forward to picking off any lookouts aboard the ship.

Rymer hopped onto the Zodiac and spat some tobacco into the water. "Don't hog them all," he said to Kresmery.

The former Army Ranger gave the Corporal a glance. "You know? If you add a little bit of detail to this skull symbol on your head, you can make it look like a bullseye."

"Maybe I should," Rymer said. "It'd just piss off whoever's trying to shoot at me, because they'll never hit it."

Serrano came aboard the boat. "Enough chatter." He looked up at the chopper and waved. Cam gave an 'ok' sign from his door gun as Lasso elevated the chopper. They knew the drill. Keep in radio contact, maintain a two-mile flight distance, and stay below radar the whole time.

He looked to the northeast. Two miles out was their target.

The team remained perfectly silent as they crossed the stretch of ocean. With the help from the stars and the tiny glow from the waxing crescent moon, they were able to make out the shape of the *Griffin.* It was eight-hundred feet from bow to stern. There were a few lights on the bridge wings, the mid deck, and the bow, providing just enough glow for the naked eye to see. From the outside in broad daylight, the vessel appeared to be like every other cargo ship. It had its company logo on the side, had steel containers secured to its deck, and moved at a leisurely pace. To any normie sailor passing by, it looked like a legit operation. Exactly what its operators had in mind.

Closer inspection confirmed either Dr. Nore or the arms dealer had some degree of paranoia. Using night-vision scopes, Kresmery and Little verified the presence of armed guards patrolling the deck.

"Got two on the portside bridge wing," Little said. "They've got rifles. Hard to say what kind, maybe AK-74s. There's likely a pair on the other side as well."

"Got three on the gangway. Bow section is loaded with containers," Kresmery said.

"So much for keeping appearances," Rymer said.

"They can justify it as being lookouts for pirates," Jarman said. "There's been some activity in this area. I'm sure the guy running this show has the money to forge the paperwork."

"Look at that," Little said. "Jarman said something intelligent."

"Nice of you to make that 'little' observation," the jarhead replied.

Little shook his head. *It never ends.*

"Can you hit 'em from here?" Serrano asked.

Kresmery scoffed. "Can Jarman get on our nerves?"

Serrano nodded. Looking through night-vision binocs, he supervised the first stage of the operation. Little took out the two men on the bridge wing while Kresmery put a round into all three sentries on the gangway.

It was time to act fast. It was only a matter of time before the next patrol stepped out. The bridge was likely minimally staffed, and whoever was there was likely not paying attention to the happenings outside.

Blake steered the Zodiac near the *Griffin's* port quarter.

Serrano was the first to ascend. Using magnetic climbing gear, he ascended the hull. Once on board, he swept the section of deck with the muzzle of his rifle. No hostiles in sight.

The rest of his team joined him on board.

"We'll go to crew quarters," Serrano said. "We should find the doctor there. We'll get in, grab him, and hit him with a sedative dart. We'll find the research, plant the charges, and get the hell out of dodge. By the time they realize something went wrong, we'll be long gone."

The mercenaries responded with a thumbs up. Understanding the next stage of their objective, the team entered the superstructure. Up the ladderwell they went, rifles aimed high all the way. They hugged the wall as they reached the passageway for the crew quarters. There was chatter coming from the other side. Two males were chuckling about something.

Serrano waited near the handle. He let his rifle hang by its sling, instead going for his knife.

The door handle turned. The crewman, speaking Russian to the other, chuckled and grabbed his crotch as he stepped out onto the ladderwell. Immediately, Serrano noticed the tattoo on the side of his neck. It was a black sickle and red droplet. This man was once part of a death squad. Maybe still was… for five more seconds, at least.

The Captain grabbed him from behind, drew his arm back, and threw the knife into the passageway. Its blade embedded itself in the center of the second man's throat. He fell to his knees, choking on his own blood and unable to unsling the rifle on his shoulder.

Crack!

In one swift motion, Serrano put an end to the first crewman. He lowered him onto the steps, his head hanging to the side, having lost the support of a neck bone.

"Whew!" Jarman mimicked wiping sweat from his forehead. *Close call.* He entered the passageway and picked up the second man's body. The ladderwell was the worst place to hide them. It was only a matter of time before another sentry would come this way. The last thing they needed was for the entire ship to awaken.

Serrano knew just where to stash them. He swept through the passageway, guiding his men toward the second officer's cabin. After checking his corners, he knocked on the door.

He heard the man inside groaning as he got out of bed. Footsteps approached the doorway.

"Izvinite menya, ser," Serrano said, using his raspy voice to mask his Western accent. He could hear the officer pulling on some pants.

The door opened, revealing a grumpy man in his upper forties. The second officer barely made eye contact before Seranno's knife plunged into his throat. Serrano forced the man into his own quarters, cupping his mouth to make sure he died silently.

Jarman and Little followed him inside and discarded the dead bodies atop their second officer.

"Do we know which room Dr. Nore is in?" Weston whispered.

"He likely has his own quarters," Serrano replied. "It should be marked on the door."

They went from room to room, checking the listing on the door. They passed the captain's quarters, the first officer's quarters, and that of the ship's chief medical doctor.

Serrano turned the corner and found the next cabin. Reading the name on the door, he gave a thumbs up to his men. *Found it.*

He knocked gently. No response. He knocked again and spoke Dr. Nore's name in Russian. Again, there was no response.

Unable to knock or speak louder without risk of drawing unwanted attention, he stepped out of the way and let Blake take over. Having done some operative work before becoming a private contractor, the merc knew how to pick a lock.

He opened the door and rushed inside, followed by Serrano and Jarman. What they found was an empty bed inside of an equally empty cabin. The blankets and sheets were neatly made, indicating the doctor had not even set foot inside for several hours.

"Oh, you've got to be kidding me," Jarman whispered.

"The doctor's probably in the lab, located in one of the cargo holds," Serrano said. "That's where we'll go—we were planning on going there anyway. But first, we'll have to take the bridge. Find their radio equipment and disable it. Take out the guards on the starboard wing. If an alarm gets triggered, we'll have a hell of a party."

With that plan in mind, they exited the cabin and went for the ladderwell. Their motion was as smooth as water, hardly producing a single sound as they closed in on the brain of the ship.

***

"Heart rate is at twelve bpm. Brachial blood pressure at forty millimeters."

Dr. Nore nodded, barely paying attention to his assistant, Diego, as he read off the vitals. He stood on the catwalk, admiring his creation down below. He could see the dorsal fin cutting across the large pool which occupied Cargo Hold Three. Almost a ton of seawater splashed as the forty-foot beast cruised in circles. Repeatedly, it had made efforts to escape. Though lacking emotion, it clearly was discontent with a life of confinement. It was a predator—a hunter—who preferred to roam the open sea and kill at its leisure. It had ignored the recent offerings gifted to it by, unbeknownst to it, its creator.

The beast cared as much for Dr. Nore as a bluegill did for a worm. It saw him only as a potential meal, with a slight awareness that this human standing above its enclosure was responsible for its imprisonment.

Nore suspected the beast had a modicum of intelligence. It was a predator driven by instinct first and foremost, but in relation to its body size, it contained the largest brain of any known species of fish. The way it explored the cargo hold supported Nore's theory of intelligence. For the duration of the trip, it did not simply idle in circles like it was doing now. It was exploring the walls and striking the bulkheads. These were not clumsy motions, but a clear effort to search for a weak point and break free. When it was unsuccessful, it resorted to its base instinct of swimming and conserving strength. The bulkheads were dented by its many violent efforts, but ultimately proved too strong for it to penetrate. A lesser ship would not fare so well against its wrath, something Dr. Nore took great pleasure with.

This fish was the first successful experiment using the Titan Serum. It was a long time coming, with many attempts leading up to it, all of which proved fatal to the subjects. Rapid mutation of the body, human or animal, was not something nature intended. Only the correct formula on the correct specimen gave any hope of success.

Up until now, his career had been spent developing new toxins, viruses, and methods of deployment, whether it was through food, air, or water. Chemical weapons were unique, for they lacked the limitations of bullets and bombs. Also, given the right method of application, they had the potential for being stealthier. A country or organization could simply hide in the shadows while the world was left in total mystery as to the cause of the outbreak.

Despite the existence of such inventions, there would always be a need for boots on the ground. Nothing short of the total extinction of mankind would bring an end to old-fashioned combat. The only thing that changed this basic reality was the technology involved, and who it was that possessed it.

It was no secret his client lacked the technological sophistication of its western enemies. Catching up would take years, even decades. And by then, those enemies would have progressed even farther. With nukes essentially guaranteeing self-annihilation, the answer for the client was to develop something new—something compatible with their method of throwing bodies at a situation.

"If you're going to use bodies, you might as well use superior bodies," Dr. Nore had said in a meeting.

The memory made him smile. The specimen below was the first major step to success. Once they arrived at the secret 'oil' facility in Somalia, he would be able to start the first phase of human trials. Should his serum prove successful, conflicts such as the war in Ukraine would see a shift in momentum.

"It's hungry," he said to Diego.

His assistant scratched his head. “We tried serving it food. We even used the acoustics to entice it. Nothing’s working.”

“It’s not a scavenger. It’s a hunter,” Nore said. “It’s not dumb. It’ll feed if it’s starving, but until it reaches that point, it has a desire to kill. It’s as though the satisfaction of taking life is as necessary a need as the physical sustenance.” It made him proud to say that, as it fed right into the plan to create genetically engineered super soldiers. If their lust for killing matched their enhanced speed, strength, and endurance, they would be unstoppable on the battlefield.

“So, what should we do?” Diego asked. “We don’t have any live prey. Considering its metabolism, at this rate, the creature may severely weaken before we get to port. Sure, it may eat then, like you said. But if Baranov sees it in an ill state, he might accuse us of failure. We refitted this boat for transport solely to get this shark over to him. If he thinks we wasted his money…”

“Hm.” Nore nodded. He continued watching the specimen, admiring it as though it were his own child. Thinking back, it had been a few days since it last fed. Its movements were a tad sluggish, indicating the effects of malnourishment. He was not as concerned with Diego’s hypothesis as he was the well-being of the fish. Like a parent to a child, he would do anything… *anything*, to make sure it was cared for. “I suppose you’re right.”

“I might be right, but that doesn’t mean there’s a solution,” Diego said. “Unless one of the guys volunteers to jump in, I don’t think there’s anything we can do.”

Dr. Nore chuckled. Diego looked over at him. It wasn’t that good of a joke. Heck, he only ever heard the doc laugh at his own jokes, or at those told by people whose asses he was kissing.

"We already have one," Dr. Nore said.

Diego paled. His mind quickly went over a few possible meanings to that statement. Clearly, he did not mean that literally. Nobody would literally volunteer to offer themselves to that thing. Unless he volunteered somebody without their knowing about it. It was sinister, but then again, that was Dr. Hank Nore. The lengths this man would go to protect his specimen had no bounds. This was the guy who ordered this ship rigged with explosives in the event of an ambush by American forces. Nore was aware that the U.S. government was tracking his every move. They may not have known the extent of his progress, but they knew what he was striving for. Hell, they wanted it for themselves.

Nothing, absolutely nothing, was going to put his creation at risk.

"I… um, who?" Diego asked. "Forgive me, Doctor, but I don't believe Comrade Baranov will stand for that. He might view his guys as cannon fodder, but that's how he intends to use them. He won't take well to the idea of you feeding them to our shark."

Dr. Nore raised a finger at his face. "Correction! First of all, it's *my* shark. I'm the one who has been perfecting this serum for four years straight, not counting the eleven years of research and development preceding that." He lowered his finger, his stern face now shifting into something more devious. "Secondly, Comrade Baranov will have no issue with whom I gift to my shark."

Diego read between the lines. His face contorted into a storm of panic and confusion. It did not come as a surprise that the doctor would sacrifice human life. He just did not expect *his*.

It was at this point the assistant was reminded of Nore's immense physical strength. Under that white lab coat was a muscular figure, forced not from scientific innovation, but sheer discipline and labor.

The doctor grabbed two fistfuls of Diego's shirt and lifted him off his feet. Though twelve years his junior, Diego could not outmuscle him. The next sensation was freefall, after that, the rush of water consuming him.

Diego floundered in the pool, shrieking as soon as he broke the surface.

"Doctor, no!"

Nore shrugged. "You said it yourself, the specimen needs sustenance. Thank you for your contributions, Mr. Perez. I can only hope your replacement will be as helpful."

Slapping water in an effort to stay afloat, Diego turned to the horrible cigar-shaped head coming at him. Drawn by his rapid heartbeat, it closed in. The need to kill was about to be somewhat satisfied.

"No… no…" Diego splashed at the gaping jaws, as though that would somehow steer them away. "NOOO!!!"

Nore watched from above as his now-former assistant was seized. Wedge-shaped teeth pierced his body, providing an exit for warm blood to cloud the pool. It shook its prey left and right, each motion producing a grunting noise from the dying human.

It whipped to the side and tightened its jaws. A snap of bone echoed behind the thrashing of water, followed by the thud of Diego's upper body hitting the bulkhead. After swallowing his lower half, the fish went to claim the rest. It had killed this meal, therefore it was worthy of consumption.

Nore smiled once more. Diego's death helped him learn something new about the creature.

It had an ego.

CHAPTER 3

All bridge crew members jumped to their feet as the door was kicked in. Serrano, Jarman, Little, and Rymer stormed the room, rifles pointed.

"Go ahead, slap leather. I dare ya," Jarman said to the four bridge crewmen. They raised their hands and kept silent.

"Keep them high," Serrano said in Russian. Two of the men had pistols strapped to their hips. The other two glanced briefly at their work consoles. Serrano was not stupid. He knew each station had a pistol stashed under the console. This was definitely not a typical cargo ship crew. The guys running this show wanted every man armed. Whatever was on this ship, they would not dare let anyone take it.

"Should we put them down?" Rymer asked.

Serrano was tempted, but the men had their hands raised. Every death up to this point served in the interest of stealth. But these guys were not resisting just yet. Shooting them would just be cold-blooded murder.

"No. We'll hogtie them and knock them out," he said. He glanced at Little and Jarman and tilted his head to the starboard wing. The men moved to the door, took position, then opened it.

At that point, one of the crewmen shouted, warning the lookouts outside.

As the door came open, the flabbergasted guards turned with their AK-74s. Jarman beat them to the punch, his suppressor muffling the cracks of double-tapping both men. Struck by a round to the chest and a second to the head, both guards slumped against the rail.

With all eyes turned to the wing, one of the crewmen took the chance of drawing his pistol. Serrano pivoted his rifle muzzle and tapped the trigger twice. Two rounds punched through the hostile, throwing him backward against the navigation console.

The other three, either out of anger or commitment to the cause, went for their weapons. Serrano swept his muzzle across the row of targets, hitting each of them right below the neckline. They fell backward, all sharing the same shocked expression as death took hold.

"Damn it, Cap," Rymer whispered. "You're hogging them all."

Serrano ignored the remark and looked through the entryway at Weston. "All clear back there?"

"So far, yes," the demolitions specialist said.

Kresmery stepped into the bridge. "Ready for me to go to work, Captain?"

"That'd be nice," Serrano answered.

Kresmery went to the main computer and took a seat. Jarman stepped over to the geek and hovered over his shoulder. "You sure you'll be able to hack into this Russian shit?"

Kresmery scoffed. "Some of us have magic tricks that actually work."

Jarman grinned, listening to some of the snorts behind him as his team suppressed laughter.

Kresmery proceeded to hack into the ship's main computer. A layout of the *Griffin* appeared on the screen, with various blocks outlining each station.

"Looks like the doctor has a lab in Cargo Hold One."

"Then that's where we're going," Seranno said. A 'hmm' from Kresmery kept him from going right to the door. "Something the matter?"

"No, I don't think so," Kresmery said. "Just, there's something about Cargo Hold Three carrying roughly five tons of saltwater. It's like they've converted that into a large pool."

"Why would they do that?" Rymer asked.

"Don't know. Don't care," Serrano said. "Let's get down there and grab Dr. Nore before any more of these assholes wake up."

He led the team in a single-file line down the corridor to the ladderwell. They passed through the superstructure of the ship, stopping at every corner to check for crew. It was like passing through the hallways of a large mansion, using signs on the walls to figure out which way to go.

They found a ladderwell which led to the lower decks. The smell of stale and rusted metal pierced their nasal cavities. The *Griffin* was showing its age and relative lack of care. The corridor lights were on, giving them a clear view of what lay ahead. It was in Deck C where they found direct passage to the cargo holds.

Cutting through the passageway, they found a door which led to the catwalks of Cargo Hold One.

They took breaching formation. Serrano looked at his men and began to count from three with his hand, only to pause as he saw Weston observing something on the wall.

"What's the matter?" he whispered.

Weston faced him, his teeth clenched, his thumb pointed at the square device tapped to the bulkhead. "Sir… that's an explosive."

That got Serrano's attention. He looked down the length of the passageway. There were several more of these black objects adhered to the seaside bulkheads. Obviously, they were not here for decoration. These guys were literally willing to explode their own ship rather than allow its contents to be taken by an enemy force.

"All the more motivation to move fast," Serrano said. "Have your fast ropes ready. Get in, knock the bastard out, swoop down, grab him, and head topside." He turned his eyes at Rymer, who loaded rubber bullets into a shotgun he had strapped on his back. The tattooed mercenary nodded, ready for action.

Serrano counted down from three, then opened the door. In they went, fanning out across the catwalk with their rifles aimed down at the hold.

Seven eyes studied the lab through the iron sights of rifles, catching no signs of human presence.

"Well, shit," Jarman muttered. It was both in reference to Nore not being present, and to what *was* present. The cargo hold was indeed converted into some kind of lab. An animal lab, to be more precise.

All across the lab were cages and aquariums containing various different species. Most of them were alive, though they probably wished they weren't. At first sight, the men could tell every single creature was in some kind of dismay, and not just from being kept in captivity. They were in physical distress.

On the left side was a cage holding a chimpanzee. Its lower jaw was crooked, its upper arms swelled well beyond its usual proportions, as if someone blew air into its biceps. Its fingers were crooked, one eye was larger than the other, and the feet were unusually large. The animal was lying on its side, barely able to move. It looked up at the men and made a few noises. Its voice conveyed the anger and agony it was in.

In the next cage was a crocodile. It too was largely deformed. Its lower jaw stretched at least a foot beyond its upper counterpart. Likewise, its legs were of different lengths, its tail stiff and bent.

There were smaller cages containing rats and mice. Even from ten feet high, the mercenaries could easily see their horrible deformities. Many of them were housed together. At some point, madness must have taken over, judging by the bloody remains smeared in the sawdust.

"Jesus," Weston muttered.

"*This* is the big experiment?!" Kresmery said. "What the hell is this psycho doctor working on?"

"I don't know, but it's enough to get the government's panties in a bunch," Little replied.

Deep in his mind, Serrano was cursing. He did not care about the findings in this lab, but rather the fact their target was not present. Time was not on their side. Every minute they remained on this ship, the more likely this mission would go to hell.

"Hurry up and plant the charges."

"These ugly bastards will probably thank us for putting them out of their misery," Jarman quipped.

"Probably," Serrano said. "Get it done, then we'll go for the pool. He's got to be there."

"What would he be doing there? Taking a swim?" Jarman muttered.

Serrano gave one last glance at the horrid mutations in this cargo hold. There were fish whose bodies were bent like corkscrews, birds with beaks almost as large as their wings, even an octopus with an aquarium with tentacles growing out of the top of its mantle.

"Whatever it is, it's related to all of this."

***

Dr. Nore proudly watched the fish resume its usual routine of circling the tank. Already, its movements were less sluggish, thanks to the snack in its belly. The 'spring in its step', as Nore described it, had returned. The beast was still hungry and eager to kill, but this recent feeding would suffice for the rest of the trip. He gave thought to sacrificing one of the animals in Cargo Hold One, but thought against it.

Can't risk an adverse reaction to those corrupted genes.

Failed projects, kept alive only for his demonstration to Comrade Baranov. In order to proceed with human trials, the arms dealer needed to know the possible outcomes. It was unclear how human flesh would react to the Titan Serum. Though what he would experiment with was different than that used on the failed specimens, there was still a chance of adverse reactions. Luckily, the success story swimming below him practically guaranteed his experiments would go forward one way or another.

The doctor moved to the edge of the catwalk, where the late Diego Perez had been monitoring the creature's vitals on a computer stationed on a desk bolted to the walkway. He clicked a few buttons on the screen, connecting him to the security feed. All he needed was one obligatory look at the specimens before he finally turned in for the night.

"Well, would you look at this!"

There was more than animals in the camera's view. Seven men, dressed head to toe in black tactical gear, stood on the catwalk with weapons pointed at the lab. His paranoia served him well. The good ol' U.S. of A was not fond of him working for a rival government. Maybe had they agreed to fund these projects, he would not have changed sides. Regardless, the government clearly wanted his expertise for themselves. Had they simply wanted him dead, they would have just sabotaged the vessel.

Though these guys were decked out in military gear, it was obvious they were not active service. With things the way they were, the U.S. did not want to be caught sending sailors onto a Russian ship. They preferred to let other countries do the fighting for them in this case. As long as the Military-Industrial Complex was making money, it didn't matter who did the dying.

Dr. Nore moved to a panel on the bulkhead. He lifted a small metal cover and activated a blaring alarm. Next to it was a speakerphone which connected to comms throughout the ship. He didn't speak Russian, but enough of the crew understood English well enough to know what to do.

"Intruder alert. Deck C, Cargo Hold One."

***

"Ah, great!" Jarman muttered.

The alert repeated itself, relaying the team's location to every single crewman aboard the ship.

Serrano looked to the upper port corner, spotting the security camera which gave away their position. Out of spite, he put a round in the device, then turned around to lead his team back into the corridor.

"Abandoning ship, boss?" Little asked.

"Yep…" Serrano loaded a fresh magazine into his rifle. "*After* we secure our target."

"Well, at least we can say this mission didn't get boring," Jarman said.

As though to make his point, the door across the cargo hold opened. Several crewmen, armed with automatic rifles, ran onto the portside catwalk. Jarman opened fire, planting a bullet through the eye socket of the first one.

Weston joined the fun, hitting two targets with rapid taps of his trigger. "Hot damn! These guys didn't waste time! I guess they sleep with their guns."

"I've got an ex-wife who does that," Jarman said, shooting another crewman.

As his men held the hostiles back with cover fire, Serrano stepped out into the corridor. Sure enough, several men were running at him from both ends of the passageway. There must have been some crewmen stationed near the bow of the ship when the alarm went off. They were prepared, carrying sidearms and rifles to the party.

Serrano unclipped a gas grenade from his vest and threw it toward the group on the aft side. White fumes filled the passageway, choking out the men on that side of the crossfire and blinding them to the next object which came bouncing their way. The fragmentation grenade burst, sending a shockwave through the condensed area. Several gunmen squawked and went silent, their bodies torn apart by the shrapnel and concussive force.

Serrano turned his weapon to the left and fired a few rounds at the other group of crewmen. They hugged the walls and backed away to take cover behind the watertight doors, clumsily returning fire. One of them was struck dead center of his chest. He looked down at the blood wetting his tank top, then dropped face-first onto the deck.

Serrano led the charge to the next compartment of the ship. Rymer, Kresmery, and Little were next to exit the cargo bay, firing several rounds into the white cloud before following their captain.

On the catwalk, Jarman was having too much fun having a shootout with the bastards opposite him. For each one he gunned down, another showed up in his place. Either they were very brave or very stupid. Or they feared the wrath of their employer more than they did the intruders.

"Come on, man," Weston said. He fired a few shots at the starboard catwalk. "Let's go, please. The others are already on the move."

He peeked out into the passageway, just in time to see a few Russians appear in the white fog to his right. He ducked back into the bay, right as a few bullets whizzed by. A moment later, he reemerged and fired several rounds with his carbine. Blood splattered from his target's naval cavity. He fired again, hitting the gunman behind the dying Russian.

Meanwhile, Jarman resumed dropping hostiles on the starboard catwalk. The fact that so many of their numbers were dropping clearly messed with their heads, for their aim was getting worse and worse. Jarman, on the other hand, barely felt his heart rate climb. For him, this was shooting fish in a barrel.

"I'm getting pissed!" Weston said. The rest of the team were already in the next compartment, working their way to Cargo Bay Two.

"Alright, alright." Laying down suppressing fire against the remaining crewmen on the starboard walk, he moved toward the door. He and Weston could hear several Russians advancing toward the door. Jarman armed a gas grenade and chucked it into the corridor, permeating the air with white fumes. Enemy crewmen coughed and gagged, clumsily firing rounds at the door.

A few shots from the starboard catwalk struck right beside Jarman's head.

"Son of a bitch!"

"Go!" Weston said, laying cover fire as Jarman made his exit. The former marine went into the passageway and fired into the smoke cloud, hearing the dying gags from his targets. He turned on his heel and moved forward to catch up with the others.

Weston stepped out, fending off the army of Russians with short, controlled bursts while backpedaling behind Jarman.

As the jarhead passed through the watertight door, he neared a ladder leading to an overhead hatch. That hatch opened. Right away, several men slid down the ladder, landing right in front of him.

Jarman struck the first one in the face with the butt of his rifle, knocking him on his back. In a fluid motion, he struck the next one, crushing his nose before putting his rifle muzzle against the chin of the third.

BANG!

The result was a gruesome one. The crewman reeled backward, dead instantly.

Jarman lifted his aim to the hatch and squeezed the trigger.

Click.

"Go figure." He drew his sidearm and fired several rounds through the hatch, repelling the next batch of henchmen. The shifting of feet in front of him drew Jarman's attention to the two Russians he floored. They were getting up and positioning their weapons.

He shifted his aim, planting three shots into one of them. Aiming a few degrees to the left, he went to shoot the other, only to realize his pistol had now run dry.

"Fuck…"

Bang! Bang! Bang!

Jarman jumped, his left ear ringing. The Russian convulsed, his chest opened up by three hollow point rounds.

Weston pushed Jarman aside and aimed his snub nose revolver to the hatch, putting the remaining three bullets into another combatant who was about to spray an AK-74 down at them.

He opened the cylinder and ejected the empty cartridges, all while glaring at Jarman.

"No such thing as a gun too small." He holstered the revolver and loaded a fresh magazine into his carbine.

"Yeah, yeah," Jarman replied. He reloaded his rifle and turned forward to catch up with the others. The intense sound of gunfire up ahead alerted them to a gridlock in the passageway. Several AK-74s discharged, their rounds striking the bulkheads and deck.

They could see the team grouped near the next watertight door. Rather than approach, Jarman used his radio.

"What's the situation up there, Captain?"

"Bit of a bottleneck," Serrano replied.

Jarman looked up at the hatch. "Hang tight. I got an idea." He faced Weston and gestured to the ladder. "Ladies first."

As Serrano neared the bow section of the ship where Cargo Bay Three was located, he was met with enemy gunfire. During the initial conflict, several men had made their way to the forecastle through the gangway and descended to Deck C by ladder.

He took cover behind some pipes and returned fire. Little took position a few feet behind him, popping off rounds at the enemy position. Rymer, Kresmery, and Blake were forced to remain behind the doorway, or else serve themselves up as easy targets in this bottlenecked space.

"Yow!!!" Little exclaimed. Serrano looked over at him, seeing his sleeve torn, the flesh underneath bleeding from a grazing wound. Little fired back, getting back at the offending Russian before he had a chance to find cover.

"At this rate, we won't have to worry about leaving witnesses," he said.

Serrano fired a burst. "Nope." He attempted to emerge from cover in hopes of gaining ground, but was immediately forced back in place.

"Bit of a clog, I might say," Rymer said.

"Hang on," Serrano said.

"What's holding up Weston and Jarman?" Kresmery asked.

"Probably showing off his precious revolver and doing magic tricks," Blake groaned.

BANG! BANG! BANG! BANG! BANG! BANG!

Simultaneous to the series of gunshots came a chorus of yelling, grunting, and the thumps of dead bodies hitting the deck. Within a few short seconds, the shooting stopped.

Serrano held up a fist, signaling to his men to remain in place. They watched with weapons pointed as two figures emerged through the watertight door.

A magic trick truly had been performed: they were relieved to see Jarman's ugly face.

"Took you long enough," Serrano said.

Jarman shrugged. "Sorry. Weston took his sweet time climbing the ladder back there. Plus, he dragged his feet walking to the next one over."

Weston stepped over the bodies of the recently slain crewmen. "I'm just glad you didn't blow us up with another grenade trick."

Serrano turned around to check the aft end of the passageway. No other crewmen were advancing from that direction. They probably wised up at this point and knew an assault would only lead to their doom.

"Let's move. Cargo Bay Three is just a few meters ahead."

***

Nore could not believe his eyes. Through the security feed, he witnessed the seven-man team of commandos eradicate the ship's security forces. He would have to have a word with Baranov about the competency of the men he hired.

That was a concern for later. Right now, the mercenaries were closing in on his position. With all of the crew either dead or cowardly retreating topside, he realized there was only one option. No way would these guys allow his experiment to survive.

In its own environment, the specimen would make short work of these men. But here, trapped in this pool, killing it would literally be shooting fish in a barrel. Its skin was resilient, but the intruders were equipped with enough firepower to get the job done. The only solution was to even the playing field.

There was only one way to do that.

Nore unclipped a smartphone from his belt. He tapped a few digital keys, syncing it with multiple receptors spread along the bulkheads of the ship. On his screen, each receptor turned from red to green, displaying the word *ARMED.*

He typed a quick message to Baranov, warning him that Plan Z was about to be initiated. It was a last-resort solution, but considering the situation, there was no other choice.

After sending the message, Nore clipped the phone back to his belt, then raised his watch to eye level. It was no typical watch. It served as a mini-computer with a speakerphone attached to it. It would ensure his own safety from the shark, provided he made it topside in time.

First, he gave the fish a look of affection, like a father admiring his child.

"Just you wait. What's about to happen might be a little jarring, but you will survive. You're stronger than anything on planet Earth. That said, enjoy your taste of freedom while it lasts. Sorry, but I'm gonna need you. You are part of something special."

The fish resumed its routine, not understanding a single word its creator was saying.

Nore backed away from the railing and took a breath. He pulled a remote device from his pocket, raised his hands, and waited for the enemy to barge in.

***

Serrano did not waste time counting to three. He opened the watertight door and stormed the catwalk. Standing forty feet in front of him was a single man. He was six-foot-two, clean-shaven, and was dressed in a typical white lab coat and business attire. His gravelly facial features and broad-shouldered physique clashed with the formal attire. Had the man been wearing typical crew clothing, he easily could have been mistaken for a gun-for-hire. Fortunately, Serrano had observed photographs of him beforehand.

This was Dr. Hank Nore.

"Figures the government would send hired guns after me," the doctor said. "You know, they had a chance to sponsor my research. But they thought it was too 'unethical'." He laughed after making the statement. "I guess at the time, they preferred things that blew people up or made them severely ill. The only biological research that interested them were viruses and bacterial illnesses. I suppose now they think different. And now, you're here."

"Not here for small talk, Dr. Nore," Serrano said. "Keep those hands up and…" He noticed the device in Nore's right hand. Immediately, his mind flashed to the explosives Weston identified on the bulkheads. "Don't you even think about it."

Nore shrugged. "Too late."

His thumb pressed down.

BOOM!!!

CHAPTER 4

Serrano fell to his hands and knees. His ears rang and his vision was hazy, both from the concussion of a nearby explosion, and the heavy turbulence of a two-hundred-thousand-ton ship in distress. The force of the blast pitched the vessel to port, threatening to throw the Captain over the railing into the pool below.

It was at that moment he realized there was more than water down there. Even with his senses jarred, he noted the odd size and shape of the fish.

The lights went dark, coating the mercenaries in blackness.

"Boss! We've gotta go!" Weston said.

Flashlights ignited, giving Serrano a view of his six men and the catwalk they stood on. Several bolts shot from place like a cork from a champagne bottle. The walkway jittered beneath their boots, threatening to toss them into the water.

Several footsteps echoed from the bow side of the catwalk. Serrano rose to his feet and aimed his flashlight, catching a glimpse of Dr. Nore as he made a turn where the catwalk connected to another one on the forward side of the bay. His athleticism served him well, his feet carrying him to the portside catwalk opposite their position.

"You guys alright?" Serrano said to his team. Beaming his light over the men, he saw six figures bunching behind him. They were flabbergasted and physically jarred, but still kicking. The bulkhead between them and the passageway absorbed the brunt of the closest explosion. Had the bombs gone off ten seconds earlier, it would have been a different story.

"We're still here," Jarman said. The sound of rushing water and groaning steel turned his attention to the passageway. The deck beneath them had also been breached, allowing the ocean to force its way in.

Dr. Nore had literally sacrificed the ship and everyone on it.

The boat leaned farther to starboard.

Going back the way they came was suicide. Their only chance was to cross the forward catwalk and make it to the port passageway and find a ladderwell.

"Time to move."

The team raced to the forward catwalk and made a left turn. Crossing over to the portside was literally an uphill journey. With the ship turning over, the catwalk was now on a thirty-degree slant.

Serrano put the guardrails to use, climbing the seventy-foot distance. All the while, he could hear the thrashing of water below him. When he finally reached the portside, he briefly aimed his light into the maelstrom below. The creature was in a frenzy. Worse, the water was *rising*. It was at that point he realized a bomb on the bottom deck had blown a hole in the side of the cargo bay.

"The hell is that?" Jarman said, looking down at it. "That a… shark?"

"You're seriously hitting the brakes on escaping a sinking ship to look at a fish?" Weston said.

Jarman shrugged. "Fair point."

Serrano found a watertight door leading to the portside passageway on Deck C. The lights here were still on, giving him a clear view of everything going on inside. The metal corridor appeared to be diamond-shaped, the starboard edge of the floor now directly beneath his boots.

On the rear end of the passageway were a crowd of crewmen. In the back of that group was Dr. Nore, feverishly trying to shove his way to the next hatch. He looked back, seeing Serrano emerging from the cargo bay.

There was a slight hint of amusement on his face, as if he was impressed with his pursuer. Still, that didn't stop him from being determined to end his life.

Nore grabbed one of the crewmen and forcefully turned him to face Serrano. "Shoot him!"

The crewman yelled something in Russian and pointed his rifle.

Serrano shot first, knocking the prick backward with a bullet to the cranium. Right then, he heard motion behind him. When the guard shouted, he was alerting a pair of sailors who were gathered near a watertight doorway between them and the ship's forecastle. They paused their escape effort for the honor of eliminating the intruders.

Serrano turned, his heart nearly leaping out of his chest when he saw their guns already pointed in his direction.

Fortunately, Jarman was already taking care of the situation. Two double-taps saved the Captain's life and spared the two hostiles from the horror of drowning.

"Ta-da!"

"Hey!" Weston said. "Can your next magic trick be GETTING THE HELL OUT OF THE WAY?!"

Grimacing, Jarman moved over so the rest could escape the cargo bay. Blake, being the last one out, slammed the door shut behind him.

Serrano led the team toward the bow. Though their target was going for a hatch in the opposite direction, there was less resistance this way. They would find Nore on the main deck and have a fresh chance at capturing him. Until then, his concern was getting out of this eight-hundred-foot steel coffin.

They reached the forecastle, where they found a ladderwell. Ascending it was an awkward process, thanks to the angle of the ship. Determination and physical agility overcame the process. In fifteen seconds, the men hurried through Deck B and emerged atop the bow of the ship.

Several spotlights had ignited on the superstructure, casting a white glow over the apocalyptic happenings on the main deck. Gravity wreaked havoc on the stacks of containers.

When empty, the steel containers weighed approximately eight-thousand pounds. Fully loaded, their weight skyrocketed near to sixty-thousand pounds. Their mass was evident in the way they fell.

Steel bodies struck one another with titanic crashes. Metal doors and sidings broke apart, spilling the contents into the water. Typical items—food, oil containers, furniture, lumber, and too many other things to count—struck the Indian Ocean.

With the deck in chaos, Serrano ordered his men to remain on the forecastle. If anything was working in their favor, it was the fact that the containers were falling directly across the deck over the starboard side.

The ship continued to teeter, forcing them to grab ahold of anchor chains and other structures in the forecastle to keep from tumbling overboard.

Serrano turned his gaze to a hatch which led to the portside gangway, which ran down the length of the ship—directly to where their Zodiac was tied.

"Follow me."

They scaled the forecastle, descended the ladder, and set foot onto the gangway. From there to the stern was equivalent to the length of two and a half football fields. In a single-file line, the mercenaries pushed themselves to the max, passing all kinds of metal textures on the pathway.

The *Griffin* shook incessantly as though caught in the grip of an angry god. Containers continued to smash against each other and into the water, the combined force of the displacement causing the ship to fishtail.

From a bird's eye view, the rotation appeared slow and steady. To those on the ship, it was like running on a bridge in the middle of an earthquake.

Running down the seemingly endless steel pathway, Serrano watched the ocean splashing against the now-exposed underside of the ship. It was now completely on its starboard side.

Weighed by the superstructure, the stern dipped first. The bow began to tilt upward. All of a sudden, the team was running down a metal slope.

It almost served as a blessing, for it helped the mercenaries increase their pace.

For every bit of good fortune came a frustrating setback.

A choir of Russian voices echoed from above. Just a few steps ahead of Serrano was a ladder leading from the top deck down to the gangway. Down came Dr. Nore, followed by three crewmen. Their goal was the same as the mercenaries'; get to that Zodiac. One of them had probably spotted it after the alarm was set off.

Nore touched down. From Serrano's perspective, the bastard seemingly materialized out of nowhere, as did the crewmen he linked up with during his escape.

Equally as surprised, the doctor shoved one of the Russians at the Captain. "Get him!"

The collision knocked Serrano's rifle muzzle to the side, forcing him to use his hands. His opponent attempted to point a pistol in his face, only to cry out as Serrano grabbed his wrist and twisted it back, directing the muzzle underneath the man's own chin.

Bang!

The crewman fell backward, the top of his head blown open.

Serrano charged, taking on the next crewman. A swift kick knocked the enemy's weapon from his grip. Serrano pressed the attack with a right-handed jab to the nose, followed by a heavy left hook. The fist struck with enough impact to send the crewman over the guardrail.

Squawking, he went over the side, flopping against the keel until hitting the water.

The third crewman, after seeing the fates of his two comrades, didn't even bother. Even if he had managed to overpower Serrano, he would simply be gunned down by the rest of his team. Figuring he was already wearing a lifejacket, he threw himself overboard to join his pal.

"Smart move," Jarman said.

Serrano directed his eyes aft, seeing Dr. Nore sprinting toward the Zodiac.

"Damn it!"

The mercenaries went after him. They crossed the halfway mark, seeing the ocean consuming the path ahead.

From the ocean came the sound of a motor and the shine from a single spotlight.

"Hey!" Weston said. "A couple of those pricks are on our boat."

Two Russians were onboard, one on the helm, the other directing the spotlight at Dr. Nore. Having unmoored the vessel from the sinking ship, they were in the middle of circling back.

"Little, you mind doing the honors?" Serrano said.

"It'd be my honor, sir."

Though Little was without his sniper rifle, he was well within range with his carbine. He put his eye to the scope and placed the dot on the man with the light. A single shot punched through the Russian's shoulder, knocking him overboard. The man on the helm turned toward the sound of splashing, then turned his eyes to the mercenaries.

"Got three seconds!" Little shouted. "Two… One…"

Abandoning the cause, the Russian threw himself overboard, leaving the Zodiac drifting unmanned.

Dr. Nore froze in place, flustered by the change in circumstance.

"Hold it!" Serrano said. The team closed in on their target. Blake and Rymer stepped forward and grabbed Nore by the arms. Serrano wasn't going to chance any more tricks. He looked to Jarman and nodded.

Knock him out.

The jarhead stepped behind the doctor and reared his rifle back, ready to strike their prisoner in the back of the head.

A deafening groan of metal reverberated through the ship. The bow tilted to forty-five degrees, then suddenly rolled farther to starboard. The *Griffin* was flipping upside down!

"Whoa!" Jarman exclaimed. He stumbled backward, nearly tumbling into the water. His fall was prevented thanks to Weston, who managed to grab ahold of his vest.

There was no time for Serrano to come up with a plan. The Zodiac was too far away and the *Griffin* was rolling too fast.

There were no two ways about it: they were going into the water.

"Brace yourselves," Serrano warned.

They had exactly seven seconds to do so. The *Griffin* completed its corkscrew, its keel now pointed to the sky, its occupants now floundering in the waves.

CHAPTER 5

A flood of stimulation assaulted every sense in the beast's impressive body. The modification of its biology gave it more than advanced strength and aggression. Every tool at its disposal was improved to three times the capacity of those of normal members of its species. Whereas a normal great white could sense a drop of blood in a mile of ocean, the titan could sense a single drop in three miles. Despite its greater size, the fish was capable of bursts of speed up to eighty miles per hour. The bite pressure from its jaw was capable of imploding the hull of a jetboat. Its lateral line picked up every square inch of motion for the surrounding mile. And its large eyes, even in darkness, were able to detect every object in a distance of two-hundred feet.

Though jarred by the intense concussions which rocked its steel enclosure, the shark quickly recovered. It did not allow itself to be flustered by the intensity of the situation. Instead, its mind and body went to work determining a method for survival.

Though the enclosure had flooded all the way to the ceiling, there was a sense of falling. An increase of water pressure indicated that the prison was sinking.

Its lateral line detected an intense current invading the cargo bay. The source of the water displacement was coming from near the bottom. As the shark closed in on the location, its eyes detected a large opening. The bulkhead had been torn open, the pieces separated into large flaps. The breach was a narrow fit, but a fit nonetheless.

Wasting no time, the shark pushed through the gap. The edges of the hull scraped its flesh, a minor price to pay for freedom.

At last, it experienced freedom. Free from the artificial structure, the shark saw the vastness of the open ocean for the first time in many years. Having achieved this goal, it immediately focused on another pressing need—the need to feed. The stress of the recent disturbance accelerated its already advanced metabolism, burning through the human snack consumed less than fifteen minutes ago. Like fueling an engine to a car constantly in motion, the fish required more flesh in its stomach. Even the miniscule effort of swaying its caudal fin back and forth burned twice as much energy than its unmodified counterparts. It was the price of its gifts.

Its senses were in overdrive, for the ocean was full of raining debris. A meteor storm of steel pierced the water and twirled to the black abyss. The dying groans of the human vessel traveled far and wide. The smell of diesel fuel flooded its nostrils, nearly motivating the fish to flee the area in search of calmer waters.

Only one thing enticed it to stay. *Multiple* things, as a point of fact. All of them were on the water's surface.

Even with the multitude of distortions, there was no mistaking the vibrations of struggling prey. Bipedal survivors, the very species who had imprisoned it for as long as it could remember, wrestled against their own weight, determined to stay afloat.

The shark had no concept of math, but it was well aware the inventory of prey was more than enough to sustain its needs for the short term. Better yet, these were *live* prey. Its bloodlust was as intense as its need for sustenance.

Both needed to be fulfilled.

With that objective in mind, the shark ascended. The only question was which human to rip into first.

***

For a few moments, Serrano wondered if a violent storm had formed overhead during their mission. Mountains of water rose and fell, carrying a field of debris and his six team members with it.

The *Griffin* completed its plunge, producing a thunderous ongoing roar which added to the illusion of being trapped in a hurricane. Its descent generated a massive suction which brought millions of gallons of ocean spiraling down, only to shoot right back up. The result was a series of giant waves tossing hundreds of pieces of wreckage.

Little by little, the waves began to settle, allowing Serrano to better assess the situation. He felt the weight of his gear doing its best to drag him down with the vessel. He looked around for any lights he could see.

Fifty feet to his ten o'clock was Jarman. The wannabe magician had taken the life vest off one of the dead crewmen and used it to keep himself afloat. To his left was Dr. Hank Nore, whose hands repeatedly slapped water in an ongoing effort to remain afloat. A fistful of his shirt was secured in Jarman's grip. Together, the mercenary and prisoner made their way to a flat piece of floating wreckage.

Jarman shoved the doctor aboard, propped himself onto the edge, and ignited a flare stick. Holding it high, he spotted Serrano coming towards him.

"Hurry it up, boss."

Serrano made his way to him and climbed aboard the piece of wreckage. "You see the others?"

"Been a little busy," Jarman said.

"They'll light flares. I'll watch for them, you watch this piece of shit." Serrano pointed at Nore. "If he tries anything, break a few bones."

Nore shook his head and smiled, amused by the Captain's devotion to his mission. Even now, with his team scattered in the middle of a raging ocean, he was single-minded in going home with the prize.

Serrano tried to stand up, only to immediately fall on his knees. The platform they floated atop of was a long sheet of plywood. A few other pieces of lumber drifted nearby, likely spilled from a container during the chaos. Baranov was probably having some construction done to whatever fortress he had in Somalia.

The sheet was twelve feet in length and three-fourths of an inch thick. It was not perfectly balanced, but at least it was able to hold the weight of the three men.

Scanning the area with his eyes, he saw a world of wreckage rising and falling with the waves. Many of the containers had burst open, many of their contents either joining the *Griffin* on the ocean floor or serving as a safe haven for the survivors up top.

A little over a hundred feet to his two o'clock was Rymer. The tattooed mercenary clung to a piece of furniture while waving a flare stick back and forth.

Three other flare sticks illuminated the darkness behind him. With the combined light of the full moon and the red tinge, Serrano was able to identify Little's significant figure. He was with two other team members, all perched atop an upside-down lifeboat originally intended for the ship's crew.

"Captain, is that you over there?" Little asked through the comm. His voice was staticky but coming through well enough for Serrano to hear.

"Got Jarman and the prize with me," he replied. "Who's that with you?"

"Kresmery and Weston."

"Rymer's in-between us. Where the hell is Blake?" Serrano asked.

At that moment, another flare lit up to their left. All eyes went to a floating piece of steel, where Blake was busy punching out a Russian crewman who dared to challenge him for the sanctuary. He waved the torch at the rest of his team.

Serrano breathed a sigh of relief. Against all odds, he and his men were still kicking. With the headcount now complete, he searched his surroundings in an effort to locate any more Russian crewmen. He couldn't have cared less if they survived, so long as they did not make an effort to attack his team.

There were three of them grouped roughly fifty feet to his six o'clock. Two of them were the fellas Serrano had thrown overboard right before the *Griffin* rolled over, the third being the guy who abandoned the Zodiac, thus avoiding getting his head blown off by Little.

Aside from them, there were three other crewmen still alive. One of them was near Blake, who was now swimming towards another pair who were huddled aboard a partly deflated raft.

"Hate to steal their idea, but we should probably be doing the same thing," Jarman said.

Serrano was about to say the exact same thing. He waved his arms to his men and pointed at Rymer's position.

"Everyone! We need to get together. Paddle towards Rymer. Don't let yourselves drift too far out. We don't want to make it too difficult for Lasso to find us."

Little's group drove their hands into the water and paddled. Little by little, they made their way to Rymer's position. The former Army corporal crossed his arms and smiled. The look on his face said it all.

Kind of nice, not having to do anything.

Jarman and Serrano scraped the water, inching closer to the Corporal. Meanwhile, Dr. Nore sat between them, watching the water. He had a strange sense of calm, as though shipwrecks were a common part of his everyday life.

"What about those other guys?" Jarman said to Serrano, tilting his head at the Russian trio behind them.

Serrano gave a glance in their direction, then immediately resumed paddling. "Nah. They're in enough trouble already. We'll keep an eye on them while we're out here, but unless they try anything stupid, let them sort out their own mess."

He gauged their distance from the others. Rymer was just a few meters ahead, and Little's group just a few meters past him.

Blake had the farthest to go. He positioned himself on the far end of his container door, kicking his feet against the water to increase speed.

Rymer leaned over and reached for their wreckage. "Hey, Cap."

"Enjoy your rest?" Serrano replied.

"I did, actually," Rymer said.

Jarman used his knife to form a small hole in the corner of the plywood sheet. He pulled a lanyard from his vest and looped it through the hole before handing the other end to Rymer, who strung it to the sofa. With the two pieces of wreckage now combined, the men awaited the arrival of the overturned lifeboat and its occupants.

As they waited, Serrano registered the sound of chuckling. He shot a glance at Dr. Nore.

"You seem awfully happy for someone who just got his ass kicked."

"You can look at it any way you wish," Dr. Nore replied.

"Believe me, I will," Jarman gladly said.

The doctor chuckled again. "Gotta hand it to you gentlemen. No life vests, all that gear you're carrying—I would've assumed you would have lost at least one man during that ruckus. But, so far, all seven of you are kicking."

Jarman snorted. "So far."

"Gotta hand it to *you*, Doctor," Serrano said. "You're not one to play around. Blowing up your own ship just to save your own skin? Seems you have a highly inflated sense of self-importance. Shame it didn't work. You've got no more friends to come to your rescue."

Nore smiled. "I wouldn't be so sure about that." He admired the waves as he spoke.

Serrano did not like the strange sense of confidence. It wasn't too uncommon for prisoners to talk a big game. In almost every single occasion, it amounted to little more than the person saving face. However, Serrano wasn't getting that impression from this guy. In a way, it made sense. The government was probably more than happy to keep him alive, maybe to utilize his skills for their own gain. But if that were the case, why would he have gone through such extreme measures to get away?

Serrano stopped. He thought of Nore's last comment. Common sense struck. Stranding himself out in the middle of the Indian Ocean wasn't going to do Nore any favors. *Unless* he had already paged a ride.

"What's the matter, Cap?" Jarman asked.

Serrano looked at the Doctor. "Got something up your sleeve? Make a radio call while you were heading topside? Unless you've got another ship within three miles of here, we'll be long gone before help arrives."

Nore's head bobbed, the expression on his face growing more jovial.

Jarman shook his head and shrugged. "He's awfully happy for a guy whose research just went down the drain."

BANG! BANG! BANG!

"Whoa!" Rymer exclaimed.

All eyes turned toward Blake. The mercenary dunked under his wreckage, only to emerge on the other side. He angled the steel door up, using it as a shield against the trio of Russians.

Armed with pistols, the idiots were actually attempting to kill the mercenary.

Serrano groaned. "You've got to be kidding me."

"Hey," Jarman said. "I asked you before…"

"Yeah, yeah, I know," Serrano said. "Should've just shot the idiots." He pulled a grenade from his vest and prepared to throw it at the raft.

SPLASH!!!

A fountain of ocean tossed the raft and its occupants skyward. Screaming, the three men flailed in midair before crashing into the water.

Rymer looked at Serrano, who still held the grenade in his hand. Obviously, it was not the source of that explosive impact.

"Uh… is this one of Jarman's magic tricks?"

"No," Little called out from the lifeboat. "This trick, whatever it was, worked."

They watched the water where the impact took place. The raft was deflated, its texture reflecting the moonlight. Not only was it deflated, but was torn into bits, as though caught in a large propeller.

Two of the Russians surfaced, gasping for breath as they desperately paddled toward Blake. Serrano unslung his rifle and took aim at them. After confirming the position of the first two, he tried to locate the third one. From what he could see, there were no signs of struggle. No splashing, no yelling, no nothing.

Jarman's brow furrowed. He wasn't sure which question to voice: "What the hell just happened?" or "Where the hell is the third guy?"

The answer to both emerged in a bloody display.

A second immense splash threw some water at the sky. This time, the cause was plain as day—even in the dark of night.

"Jesus…" Serrano muttered.

A damn shark. It kept its head pointed at the sky, as though proudly displaying the catch snagged in its jaws. The third crewman writhed, his midsection flayed open by the multiple rows of wedge-shaped teeth. Slapping its chin against the water's surface, the fish thrashed its head back and forth.

There was one final grunt, followed by the splashing of the man's upper body being thrown clear of those teeth. The shark moved slowly, as if unsure whether to consume the rest of that meal, or investigate the sounds of two other panicked men splashing in the water.

It chose the latter option.

Serrano watched the beast as it moved. There was no doubt in his mind it was the same beast he had seen inside Cargo Bay Three. It was at least forty feet in length, had skin that was lined with what appeared to be thorns and bumps, and had smooth black eyes which reflected the light of Blake's freshly-lit flare.

A hellish demon, it closed in on the Russians.

Like a monstrous bear trap, those jaws slammed shut over one of the men, encompassing his entire left side. There was a brief mixture of grunting and snapping bones before the teeth intertwined. The rest of the crewman 'popped' from the jaws. The head, right shoulder, right ribcage, and right hip all remained attached, forming a bizarre crescent-shaped corpse which drifted with the waves for a few meters.

The third Russian, stricken by the vile sight of his dead comrade, backstroked toward Blake's wreckage. He shouted in his native language, though only the tone was understood by the nearby mercenary. Even if Blake wanted to, there was nothing he could have done except watch as the dorsal fin cruised toward the Russian.

The jaws emerged, fully parted, pieces of fabric dangling from the white triangles. A bloodcurdling scream traveled far and wide. The Russian reared back, lifted high as the fish reared its head several feet over the surface. A fierce hunter, it almost appeared to take pleasure in the death it caused—a theory supported by its next action.

It slammed its head forward, bringing the Russian's skull against the edge of Blake's wreckage. The result was a gruesome spectacle which made even the hardened mercenary look away. Bits of brain splattered against the edge of the door, soon washed away by waves of water.

The fish turned away, its tail smacking the door as it munched on the remains.

After a few short moments, that dorsal fin reemerged.

"Good God!" Weston said. "It's a freaking shark."

"Hungry ass shark," Kresmery added. "It's going after everyone. That's not normal."

"Oh, and I suppose you're an expert," Little replied.

"No, but all it takes is a little internet research," Kresmery said. "Even if this shark was intent on eating humans, it would have stopped after the first one."

"You suggesting this is not a normal shark?" Little said.

"Uh, have you not noticed how big that thing is?" Jarman said.

"It's a little dark out here," Little replied.

"Shut up," Serrano said. He cupped his hands over his mouth. "Blake! Throw your flare away!"

The merc did as instructed, tossing the flickering red stick as far as possible. The shark turned and moved in on the light, losing interest once the flames died out.

A swing of its tail kicked up water. Using its burst of speed, the shark moved in on a new point of interest.

Serrano quickly lost the fish in the darkness. However, it immediately became clear where it had gone.

A choir of screaming and splashing illustrated the demise of the *Griffin's* last three crewmen. From Serrano's position, he could only catch a few large waves sparkling in the moonlight. It was more than enough as far as he was concerned.

The screams degenerated into a blend of grinding, retching, and wet tearing sounds. It created a horrible mental image of the three men being caught in a giant food processor.

Even after the sounds of agony had ceased, the fish ravaged the water, likely feasting on any remains it could find.

The seven mercenaries waited in silence. Those who weren't watching the water were now looking at Dr. Nore.

Serrano exhaled slowly. The cocky expression on the doctor's face made sense now.

Blake stood on his knees, balancing himself on the wobbly plate. Water dripped from his night vision binoculars as he aimed them at the sounds of chaos. Zooming a few hundred feet, he caught a glimpse of a large crescent-shaped tail fin splashing water warmed by the blood of three men.

Rolling with the waves was a cluster of scraps. Remains. Arms, legs, clothing… a human head which seemed to stare right back at the glasses right before sinking to the ocean floor.

In the middle of it all was that huge dorsal fin. No doubt, this shark was a product of Dr. Nore's experimentation. Whatever the jackass did, it resulted in a hyper-violent beast.

Blake panned back and forth. From what he could see, there was only one shark. He turned the glasses back to the threat. Having circled the kill zone five or six times, the shark moved on. Its dorsal fin sliced westward, seemingly heading toward Africa before suddenly turning north. Towards him.

"Son of a bitch," he muttered.

His captain's voice came through his headset. *"Blake. Keep quiet. Don't move."*

Blake tapped his microphone to rid it of any water droplets. "Don't think that's gonna work, sir. It seems to know exactly where I am."

As he spoke, the shark gradually picked up speed.

An idea formed in his mind. Obviously, the fish was attracted to light. With that in mind, he ignited another flare stick and tossed it forty feet out. The burning stick glistened as it pierced the waves. The fish, stimulated by the red glow, angled to its right to investigate.

Blake shouldered his rifle. The fin was in plain sight now, thanks to the illumination from the flare.

"Blake, what are you doing?" Serrano asked.

"Sir, it's a mean ass fish—but at the end of the day, it's still a fish. Equally killable."

He put the dorsal fin in his scope, then moved slightly to the left to aim at the shark's head. A squeeze of the trigger sent three bullets zipping at the cigar-shaped target. The fish jolted as though struck by a bolt of lightning, rolling over on its side, and angrily smacking the water with its caudal fin.

Blake switched his weapon to full-auto and resumed the punishment. The shark writhed along the surface as a stream of bullets punched its underside. While Blake was uncertain of the amount of damage he was causing, the physical reaction of the shark sparked a sense of triumph within him. It seemed awfully clear he was winning this fight.

The magazine ran dry, forcing him to eject it and slam a fresh one in its place. He hit the shark with another dozen rounds before it disappeared beneath the rolling swells.

Blake took his finger off the trigger. The water gradually calmed, offering no signs of the beast. Keeping the rifle shouldered with his right hand, Blake raised his binocs to his eyes. Through the electronically enhanced glasses, he saw nothing but rippling sea.

Gently, he rose to his feet. Balancing as though standing on a surfboard, he resumed his search.

A sense of victory began to well up within him.

"I've lost visual," Serrano said through the radio.

Blake was smiling now.

"Don't worry, sir. I think I got it." He spat into the water and laughed. "Sorry, Doc! I guess I ruined your science project."

SPLASH!

Blake's laugh turned into a fright-fueled holler. A force of nature and science combined into one horrifying cone-shaped monstrosity, the shark threw itself at the target. Its enemy's assault had merely scratched its flesh and fueled its desire for murder.

Its chin crashed down against the edge of the door, driving the other side upward, catapulting Blake straight into its open jaws. What came next was a hurricane of agony as three-inch teeth were driven into his lower back and abdomen.

"Goddamnit," Serrano exclaimed. He, Jarman, and Rymer took aim with their weapons and fired at the shark's exposed hide. Their combined assault did little but prick its thick skin while it ravaged their brother-in-arms. Blake was still alive, his legs kicking outside of those closed jaws.

They tensed as the grip tightened, the muffled screams still audible from the back of the creature's throat. The fish turned to its right, facing the rest of the team. As if to inflict psychological warfare, it proceeded to munch on Blake right in front of them.

It chewed on him as one would gnaw on a slab of beef jerky, reducing his physical structure to a soft piece of fleshy mulch. Its impact, whether intentional or happenstance, struck the hearts of each team member. The legs fell free, their stubs soft and comprised of strands of meat which almost resembled tendrils.

A fresh volley of gunfire struck the shark in the face. Though failing to penetrate its spiny flesh, it was enough to drive the shark away for the time being. It bent its body, performing a sharp turn. A heavy swing of its caudal fin generated a large splash. When the curtain of water fell, the fish was gone.

Jarman wasted no time pressing the muzzle of his rifle against the back of Dr. Nore's head.

"You psycho motherfucker."

Nore responded with a derisive chuckle. "You're pissed at me? Hate to break it to you, but nobody invited you aboard this ship."

Jarman looked to Serrano. *Please, PLEASE, let me shoot this son of a bitch.*

Serrano was quiet, partially tempted to give in to the temptation. As long as they offered proof of the doctor's death, the client would not be too pissed. After consideration, he decided the best revenge would be completing the job. Better yet, for Dr. Nore to witness the death of his beloved pet before being hauled back to the states.

The shark was fierce and durable, but it was still just a shark. If a certain weapon was insufficient in neutralizing a target, the solution was to go with a higher caliber.

“Keep him secured,” Serrano said to Jarman. He turned to Little, who was in the process of securing the lifeboat to their assembly of wreckage. “Get on the horn. Tell Lasso to get his ass over here, and make sure Cam is on the gun. He’s earning his pay tonight.”

CHAPTER 6

"Uh, could you say that again, Little?"

"You heard me right the first time, Lasso. Get your ass over here. Keep your lights off until you get over here."

"You're telling me there's a shark stalking you guys?"

"It's not any ordinary shark. It's connected to the research our prisoner was involved in," Little said. *"It killed Blake. After you pick us up, we're going hunting. It's payback time."*

Lasso pursed his lips. He knew it was a matter of time before they would lose somebody. In this business, it was inevitable. But to a monster shark? That was the last thing he expected to hear.

"On our way." He turned the chopper thirty degrees starboard and increased speed. "Cam, you catch all of that?"

"Heh!" It was all the gunner had to say. He didn't care who or what his target was, just as long as he got to shoot something. Since this enemy was responsible for taking the life of one of his teammates, killing it would be all the more satisfying.

It only took a quick minute for the chopper to reach the destination.

Lasso activated the forward spotlights. Large white beams reflected the ocean's surface. The *Griffin* was gone, leaving a floating landfill in its wake.

"Hey! Did you not listen? No lights," Little said.

"How the hell am I supposed to find you?" Lasso replied.

"Use your eyes. You can't miss us."

"Ugh."

Cam swiveled the door gun, resisting the urge to use his own spotlight to search for the team. He could see objects below, but in this dark, he struggled to identify what they were.

It wasn't long before he noticed a blinking light coming from the east.

"That way," he said to Lasso.

The pilot saw it too. One of the guys was using a flashlight to signal their position without attracting the shark. He turned the chopper to port and closed in on the source.

There they were, bunched together on some wreckage.

"Is that a couch?" Lasso said.

"I think it is," Cam shouted.

Lasso lowered the bird to twenty feet and held position. Cam dropped a rope ladder to the team and waited by the door gun.

Dr. Nore sat cross-legged, watching the mercenaries fumble on the stupid sofa while trying to grab the ladder. The nonstop gust from the rotors threatened to push the makeshift platform away. After a few bumbling attempts, the one named Little managed to get ahold of it.

"Looks like you've made the lucky draw," Serrano said to him. "Climb on up. Move along. We don't have time to linger. Rymer, hold on to the ladder so we don't lose it."

Not one to irritate the boss, Little began his ascent. Kresmery grabbed ahold of the bottom ladder bar, more than happy to follow him up.

Nore felt Jarman's hand clutching his shoulder. The mercenary was ready to shove him toward the ladder. It was the only degree of abusive force he was allowed.

"You guys are next," Serrano said.

Jarman exercised that force, shoving Nore toward the sofa. The doctor played up the role of a victimized prisoner, falling on his hands and knees with a pitiful cry.

In this face-down position, he nonchalantly glimpsed at his wristwatch. To the men around him, it was nothing more than an expensive Apple watch. It didn't have much to offer other than a one-inch screen and a few buttons. None of them noticed the speaker on top, and even if they did, they probably assumed it was a speaker for a wrist communicator.

Nore eyed the tiny square button on the top left side of the monitor. Engraved in the metal were the letters *LF*.

Low Frequency.

"Come on, Doc. Quit being such a baby," Jarman said.

"Sorry, I—whoops!" Nore fell forward again, having 'lost his balance'. His thumb brushed over the button, activating the low frequency signal, right before his right hand dipped into the water.

Jarman grabbed him by the back of his shirt. "Wow. This is pathetic. Where'd the confidence go, *Frankenstein*?"

Nore looked at the water and smiled. "I've got it right here." He retracted his hand and threw himself into the middle of the group.

SPLASH!

A towering wall of water preceded the emergence of the mutant shark. It rose to the sky like a surface to air missile, unsure whether to focus its attack on the flying machine or the easier prey on the surface.

The pilot's exclamations could be heard even without the aid of radio. Instinct kicked in. He yanked on the joystick, veering the bird sharply to port. The shark's dorsal fin grazed the landing struts as it passed underneath. It vanished under the waves, the resulting splash throwing large droplets at the fishtailing chopper.

Little, Rymer, and Kresmery clung to the ladder for dear life. The latter two quickly lost their grip and were flung into the debris field.

The fast maneuver put the chopper into a spin, a sight which brought much joy to Dr. Nore. At some point, the door gunner activated his spotlight, probably to help relocate the two lost men.

His mind's eye could envision his creation closing in on the white glow.

Three... two... one...

The shark breached directly under the chopper. Its jaws closed over the ladder, pulling it toward the water. The chopper whined as the pilot attempted to pull up; the man on the ladder gasping as he gazed at the snout less than a foot under his boots.

There was a tearing sound, then a colossal splash. The chopper climbed and spun, its ladder torn where the shark had bitten it. During the fishtailing, the large man comically referred to as Little finally lost his grip. His splash was barely audible under the chatter of Jarman and Weston and the slicing of rotors against the air.

Its pilot regained control once again. This time, he activated his forward spotlights and circled to the west.

"Alright, now I'm pissed. I'm drawing it away from you. Cam's on the gun. Once it comes up again, we'll carve it like a Thanksgiving turkey."

"Be careful," Serrano replied.

As the chopper moved away, Serrano, Weston, and Jarman combed the waters with their eyes in search of the other team members.

Weston pointed north. "I see Rymer and Kresmery."

Thirty feet out, the two mercenaries were clutching onto a floating board. It was not enough for them to haul themselves out of the water, but it was enough to keep them from sinking.

"Anyone see Little?" Serrano asked.

The sound of splashing and screaming turned their attention forty yards left of Rymer and Kresmery's position. Pistol shots echoed, then the sound of something enormous and heavy landing on the water.

The chopper's door gunner must have heard this too, for he finally activated his spotlight. Cam panned the thick white beam left and right, scanning the seascape until finding the ripples of rapid movement.

It emerged in the glow, holding the large mercenary in its jaws. Little was completely in its mouth, the teeth impaling his upper chest and back. Just like before, the beast appeared to be showing off its kill to the others, chomping Little, deliberately making his death slow and painful.

Gushing blood from his mouth, the mercenary continued to fight. He had his sidearm pressed against the shark's snout, firing point blank. Even then, it did not cause any damage.

The shark carried its victim several yards across the surface. From its gills came red water pigmented with Little's blood. The mercenary reared his head back and let out one last gurgle, which was punctuated by a nauseating *crunch!*

His head, arms, and shoulders fell free, leaving the rest to be vacuumed into the creature's gullet.

Nore watched as the fish immediately pointed its snout at Rymer and Kresmery. Even after killing the team's strongest member, the fish was not satisfied. It wanted nothing more than to add to its body count.

The doctor never had kids, but he always wondered what it felt like to be a proud parent. Today, he got his answer.

Slaying its victims gave the shark more than sustenance. It provided satisfaction. It sought out live prey because it felt the thrill of the sport. Truly, this beast was a hunter at heart.

Machine-gun fire broke his concentration. The shark veered sharply to the left, its advance on the two mercenaries cut short.

The helicopter returned from the west after witnessing the second casualty. The door gunner kept his spotlight and machine-gun centered on the dorsal fin, stinging his target with fifty-caliber rounds.

Each hit spurred the shark further. It raked the ocean with wide swings of its caudal fin, doubling its speed. The floating victims could wait for later. Right now, the shark was focused on taking on this aerial threat.

"Come on, fishy-fishy," Lasso said. For the second time, he steered the bird west. This time, the shark was following him.

When Little had informed him about a killer shark in the water, Lasso was certain it was an exaggeration. A shark in the middle of the ocean was not far-fetched in and of itself, but a *giant mutant* shark capable of eating multiple people within minutes? Even with the news of Blake's death, the description seemed too ridiculous to be true.

Yet, here it was. With its immense size came unmatched aggression. The shark was actually coming after the helicopter. Worse, it did not appear as though the machine-gun was causing any significant damage. Even as bullets pelted the top of its head, the shark kept coming.

"This is just ridiculous," he said. "Up till now, I thought I'd seen it all."

"Maybe you'd like to see a forty-foot shark blown up by missiles," Cam said.

Lasso nodded. "After what it did to our guys, I could go for that."

He continued leading it west, whilst keeping an eye on Serrano's position. The Captain had gone ahead and lit a flare stick, allowing Lasso to gauge the distance between them.

After six hundred feet, he elevated the chopper and armed the missile pods. Hellfire missiles, designed to bring down enemy strongholds, were primed and ready to turn the fish into chowder.

He put both forward spotlights on the target, giving him a clear view of the details of its body. It swam in tight circles, angling the side of its head upward to keep its eye fixed on the chopper. Its actions were as strange as its size and physical features.

The fish was actually watching the chopper and monitoring its actions. Lasso was no marine scientist, but he knew that was not normal. Nor was its physical design.

What caught his eye most were the strange spines lining its flesh. Each one was almost a foot in length, their tips sharp enough to skewer a man. They were all over its body, with a shockingly large grouping on its tail fin. The damn shark was practically an aquatic porcupine.

Probably a defense mechanism. Lasso smirked. *Too bad it won't help against what I've got in store for it.*

He attempted to lock onto the shark, only for the targeting system to fail.

"Can't lock on to it," he said. "Fish isn't warm enough. That's fine. I'll eyeball it."

Right then, the shark dove, obscuring itself underneath multiple layers of water.

Four missiles launched, trailing thick lines of smoke. They struck where the target had been circling, instantly producing a combined burst of flame, shrapnel, and water. The ocean convulsed, the top layer of water cratering for a brief second before rebounding with force equal to the missiles. A ring of mini tsunamis expanded from the blast area. Though the pilot and gunner could not see it, the sea beneath those waves was simmering as the shockwaves tore into the depths.

Lasso held position, sweeping the kill zone with his lights. In the minute which followed, he saw nothing but smoke.

"I don't have a visual," he said.

"Same here," Cam said.

Lasso flew the chopper for a radius of a few hundred feet. The ocean was calm now, with nothing but floating remnants of the *Griffin* in sight. Anything unfortunate enough to be caught in the blast was currently sinking to a watery grave.

He completed three passes, with no sign of the fish.

"Anything?" he called to Cam.

"Negative," the gunner replied.

Lasso smiled. "I think we got him."

Both men celebrated with laughter. Vengeance was theirs.

"Christ alive!" Serrano shouted through the radio. *"Lasso, get back here NOW! The shark double-backed and is attacking."*

"What the—" Lasso felt confused and cheated. The shark was still alive? How the hell was it still alive?

His mind flashed to the split-second before he opened fire. The shark had sped out of the blast area right before he fired. In the moments prior to that, it watched as he ascended to a safe firing distance.

Son of a bitch. It knew something was up.

He turned east and returned to the team.

Serrano pivoted to the right. The damn dorsal fin had emerged. The fish was just a few meters away, exposing its hide. Swimming in rapid circles, it caused their wreckage to spin in place.

Jarman and Weston hit it with a few bursts, driving it back under the water. Before they could catch their breath, it had already emerged once again, this time on the other side of their wreckage.

The shark turned its head and snapped at the edge of the plywood sheet. Serrano hit it with a few shots before throwing himself onto the middle of the sheet. Its snout struck the corner, sending the sheet and its occupants into a brief spin.

Jarman fired a few shots at its caudal fin, which whipped water as the shark began to make another pass.

"The hell's it doing?" he asked.

Serrano shook his head. At this point, it was anyone's guess what the fish was trying to do. Even Dr. Nore was watching with fascination. It was as though the shark was only making half an effort in its attack.

"Maybe it's full," Weston said.

"Don't think it cares," Jarman replied.

They turned to the sound of helicopter rotors.

Serrano lit another flare and tossed it at the shark's position. It went at the light, stopping briefly to admire it. The Captain tilted his microphone to his lips, ready to update Lasso on the situation. Before he could mutter a single syllable, the shark threw itself at the door.

It grabbed ahold of the corner. This time, it was not letting go.

All four men grabbed onto whatever they could to keep from falling into the water. Their floating sanctuary was being dragged alongside the fish. Even with the weight in tow, it was reaching speeds of twenty knots.

"Okay, this is not cool!" Weston shouted.

The chopper followed overhead, planting a spotlight on the raft.

Right then, the shark let go. It kept going for another several yards before doubling back.

Serrano sat up and watched it steer close to the raft. The way its head angled up…

"It's using us for cover," he muttered. "It knows Lasso won't use rockets near us."

"Wait a sec," Jarman said. He waved a hand, settling himself down from the unpleasant ride and also trying to grasp what Serrano was trying to say. "You're suggesting it's holding us hostage?"

"Using us as a human shield, to be more precise," Weston added.

"It's a shark!" Jarman said. He laughed, not from amusement, but recognizing the ridiculousness of this scenario. Whether the shark had truly planned this or not, the result had been achieved. Lasso could not fire any missiles or rockets with it so close to them.

"Is this what the government wants with you, Doctor?" Weston said to Nore. "They have a 'genetically engineered killer shark' program or something?"

"Like it matters," Jarman said. "So what if it's using us as human shields. What's it gonna do? Shoot back?"

Large droplets struck his face, shutting him up.

The shark slapped its tail on the water, turning itself perpendicular to the Seahawk. It raised its tail, not in a swimming motion, but up and to the side, similar to a scorpion when striking. The first two movements were slow and tense. Then came the third motion. It was fast, the fin whipping towards the cockpit.

Serrano noticed a streak of motion, like a shooting star, zipping from its caudal fin. At the same time, his ears registered the unmistakable sound of a large projectile striking the hull of the Seahawk.

The chopper went into a tailspin, the mast of its main rotor squealing as the blades continued to keep the machine airborne.

The shark whipped its tail again. This time, Serrano got a clear visual of its secret weapon. A twelve-inch thorn spat from its caudal fin like a bullet. There was the sound of shattering glass, unmuffling the sounds of Lasso cursing within the cockpit.

Alarms rang out. Fuel pressure dropped. The rotors threatened to stop spinning. All the while, the chopper itself *refused* to stop spinning.

Lasso yanked on the joystick.

"Climb, baby, climb…"

It didn't.

Lasso watched the water get closer and closer. He could not believe it. The shark had actually used Serrano and the others as bait, setting him up for a projectile strike.

I was outsmarted by a goddamn fish!!!

His efforts to keep the Seahawk airborne had failed. It crashed bow-first, the rotors snapping on contact with the ocean. Razor-sharp fragments tore through the air, threatening to decapitate his nearby team members.

Water rushed into the cockpit.

Lasso freed himself from his harness and reached for the cockpit door. Looking out the window, he caught a glimpse of a massive torpedo-shaped object racing at the fuselage.

CRASH!

The Seahawk juddered, throwing Lasso against the console. Repeated sounds of crashing reverberated through the fuselage. Pistol shots rang out, preceding a sound Lasso never thought he would ever hear.

Cam, the silent mercenary who only spoke when necessary, who had taken six bullets and three pieces of shrapnel in his combined military and private service—screamed in a way that could only be caused by unbearable pain.

Lasso righted himself and opened the door. The chopper remained afloat, leaning heavily on its starboard side.

Looking to his left, he saw the shark's body protruding from the fuselage. The door gun had been ripped off its mount and lost to the sea. Cam's screams persisted, as did the pistol shots… until the magazine ran dry, that is.

Whipping its head, the shark freed itself, holding Cam horizontally in its jaws. The teeth dug deep, inflicting all kinds of bodily damage. In one single chomp, he suffered deflated lungs, a lacerated stomach, broken bones, castration, and ruptured kidneys all at once. The screaming stopped, not for lack of trying. Blood jetted from the gunner's mouth.

His killer froze in place, its superior senses detecting movement from the cockpit. It tilted its head a few degrees left, pointing its eye at the pilot. All of a sudden, its interest in Cam vanished. It tossed the now-dead gunner aside, his body breaking apart as it skidded on the waves.

Lasso shrieked as the fish came at him. He threw himself at the cockpit and reached for his sidearm. In doing so, he nearly escaped those horrible jaws. Nearly.

He gasped as a serrated-edged object sawed his ankle bone. In the blink of an eye, he was yanked out of the cockpit and dragged along the water. The shark had him by the foot, its bite pressure just shy of severing it at the ankle.

This bastard shark was doing this on purpose.

"Fuck… ah!" He spat water as he shouted. "Fuck… you! You stupid guppy! You freaking psycho fish!"

Despite its intelligence, the shark did not understand a word he said. Even if it did, it wouldn't care. It was still bound by instinct, just like normal sharks. But normal sharks had an instinct to kill strictly for survival.

The mutant's instinct drove it to kill. Period.

It let go of Lasso. Floundering in the waves, he made another attempt to unholster his pistol. The shark continued, slowed, bending its tail sharply to the right. Like the hammer of a revolver, it sprang the other direction. Right toward him.

SMACK!

Lasso was knocked clear of the water and splattered against the hull of his helicopter, decorating it with his guts.

"Oh, Jesus!" Jarman exclaimed. All sense of military discipline threatened to leave him. He was on all fours, on the verge of dry heaving.

"Snap out of it," Serrano said.

Though he would not admit it, he was barely holding himself together. He had lost men before. It was inevitable in this business. But he rarely lost more than one in a single mission. Four years ago, on a mission in Columbia, his team suffered two casualties. He remembered that being a rough day.

This morning, in the span of minutes, he had lost four guys. Worse, their ride was gone, and the rest of his men were stranded in the ocean, miles from land, with a bulletproof sea monster stalking them.

Maintaining the exterior façade of a leader in full control of the situation, Serrano allowed himself a brief moment to come undone internally. Only three words screamed in the depths of his mind, summing up his day.

Fuck this mission.

As much as he wished he could snap his fingers and teleport he and his men onto dry land, he had to face reality. They were here, whether they liked it or not. With that in mind, he had to come up with a new solution. Giving up was not an option, no matter how high the odds were stacked against them.

"It is a perfect specimen," Dr. Nore announced. He spoke as though hundreds of cameras were on him. The tone of his voice represented an ego so large, it was rivaled only by the shark's aggression. "You have picked a fight you cannot win. I have taken the ultimate killing machine and enhanced it with scientific innovation. You see, this shark holds the key to the next stage in human development. It is my Titan Prototype—the first of many successful experiments. Soon, once the rest of you are dead, I will conduct human trials. Before long, I will breed a superior race."

"Funny," Weston said. "I remember reading about some German guy with a funny mustache desiring the same thing."

"Joke all you want," Nore said. "Maybe the flippancy will make your deaths less terrifying."

Now, Serrano felt the temptation to put his gun muzzle to the idiot's temple and squeeze the trigger. To hell with the objective.

Some inner force compelled him not to do it. There was no rational thought behind it, other than a feeling of the time not being right. Sure, killing the guy would put his future plans to a halt, so there was victory there. But the guy would still die knowing he had beaten Serrano.

Perhaps Serrano was developing something of an ego himself. As he had decided before, he would kill the shark in front of its creator. Only then would Nore truly suffer the consequences of playing God. The guy was a freak, looking at the shark with loving eyes. Killing the shark would be like killing his next of kin. Never in a million years would Serrano ever kill a child. Fortunately, he had no reservations about killing an overgrown fish. Especially if it gave this asshole some grief.

The shark, drawn by the scent of Lasso's blood, swam to the Seahawk. It investigated the aircraft, making sure there were no other occupants to slaughter.

"Damn thing sure is thorough," Weston said.

"Yes, it is indeed," Nore replied. "As you will find out firsthand."

The shark nudged the chopper, inadvertently turning its bow toward the mercenaries. Extending from the water was the port rocket pod, fully loaded.

Serrano perked up. An idea had come to mind.

"Weston? How good is your throwing arm?"

"Uh..." Weston mimicked throwing a baseball. "Good, I guess."

Serrano ignited a flashlight and aimed it at the rocket pod. Immediately, Weston understood what he had in mind.

With an enthusiastic "ah-ha!", he dug an explosive charge from his vest.

Dr. Nore propped himself on his knees, his gleefulness gone. In its place was a display of apprehension. He was not stupid—he, too, knew what they were planning to do.

"Don't you dare!" He threw himself at Weston. The demolition expert stuck his tongue out as Nore's arm formed a crushing chokehold around his neck. The lab coat had fooled them. This doctor was not simply some science nerd who spent all of his time in the lab. He was built like a shit brickhouse, displaying an iron grip fueled by a raging attitude.

Jarman pointed his rifle, only for the crazed doctor to slap it away. Pushing Weston onto the sofa, Nore turned his attention to Jarman, successfully landing a powerful haymaker to the chin. With the jarhead on his back, the doctor turned to take on Serrano.

The Captain had no interest in fighting fair. By the time Nore faced him, he was already lunging with the butt of his rifle. He struck the doctor right between the eyes, stunning him enough to hold him still for a second blow. This time, Serrano struck him in the jaw.

Weston, gritting teeth, gave him the third and final strike. The butt of his weapon connected with the back of Nore's head, sprawling him across the plywood sheet.

Serrano immediately looked to the chopper. The shark had completed its investigation and was in the process of moving away.

"Weston! Throw the charge! Hurry!"

Realizing the window of opportunity was closing fast, Weston picked up his charge, armed it with a five-second timer, then chucked it at the aircraft. The bomb arched through the air, landing less than a yard shy of the rocket pod.

BOOM!

BOOM-BOOM-BOOM-BOOM!!!

The explosion set off the rockets, which exploded with the rhythm of Fourth of July firecrackers. Their combined concussion went far and wide, catching the shark off guard. Caught in the shockwave, it rolled like a massive wheel, its jaw slack.

Shrapnel protruded from its thorny hide, its blood seeping into the ocean. With its tail stiffened, the shark sank beneath the waves.

Despite the pounding in his head, Serrano kept his light fixed on the shark, even as it sank. There was no room for uncertainty. He *needed* to know if the damn thing was finally dead.

"Hey, HEY!" Jarman shouted.

Dr. Nore scampered on all fours toward Serrano. The Captain grabbed for his rifle, ready to crack it against his prisoner's skull once again.

Nore paid him no mind, as fighting was not on his agenda at the moment. He settled on the edge of the wooden sheet beside the Captain and gazed into the water. Breathing heavily through his mouth, he forced Serrano's flashlight back into the water. He, too, needed to know the shark's condition—though for different reasons than Serrano.

Together, they viewed its elongated shape through the distortion of waves. It was twenty feet down, its white underside facing up. Stiff as a brick, it gradually sank out of view.

Serrano looked to the doctor. "Say goodbye to your perfect specimen." He stood up carefully, then made his way toward the lifeboat, leaving Dr. Nore to sulk.

Nore kept his gaze fixed on the water, playing the part of the defeated scientist whose greatest experiment was destroyed. In doing so, he kept an eye on his watch. Its design was simple, not meant to draw attention from others—a choice which proved most useful.

Angling the small screen toward his face, he checked the readings sent from the shark's implant. Its blood pressure had fallen but was stabilizing. Its heart rate nearly flatlined but was gradually increasing.

A superior being, it refused to die. At the moment, it was stunned and would need a period of time to recover. Knowing the beast, though, it would not let this fight go unfinished. Only death would seal the outcome.

He forced himself not to smile, as the display of confidence would certainly alert the mercenaries to the truth. The expression of joy would come later. For now, he chose to let Serrano and his men believe they had killed the shark.

Jarman and Weston slapped hands, the former throwing insults at Nore's expense.

Those words, meant to serve as a knife piercing into Nore's ego, only expanded the exultant sentiment in his heart.

Let these guys celebrate. Pride cometh before the fall.

CHAPTER 7

The creature feared nothing. Not even the echoes of apocalyptic collisions. Like a meteor from beyond the stars, the gargantuan object struck the seabed, instantly forming a crater four meters deep. A thick storm of silt had risen around the eight-hundred-foot steel beast, forcing away any lifeforms unfazed by the thunderous soundwave.

In a matter of seconds, this region of the ocean floor became a barren wasteland, peppered by shards of metal and other inorganic material which spread like volcanic ash around the wreckage. Fuel and other odors, all of which were unidentifiable to the simple-minded lifeforms of the deep, permeated the water. The strains of pollution instantly took effect on much of the sea life within range. Though they couldn't see it in the darkness, a black cloud seeped through the silt storm, permanently tarring the gills of any fish who chose to investigate. Those who didn't suffer immediate respiratory complications fled the area.

Only one lifeform remained.

To the land-based world, it was known as Architeuthis Dux. In the animal world, it had no name. Its only purpose; one which was shared by every other living thing in the sea: Survival.

A three-year-old adult, it had grown to a mantle length of six feet and a tentacle length of thirty-two feet. Adept in both the shallows and deep ocean, it was an experienced hunter and scavenger. Whilst the giant squid had slain more than its fair share of prey in its lifetime, the latter method proved easier and expended less energy.

Undeterred by the pollution and shockwaves, it pierced the cloud of silt and oil. The structure at the center of this storm was man-made. The squid had witnessed such large vessels in operation, always floating atop of the water despite their incredibly large mass. Now trapped hundreds of feet down, the machine was motionless. In time, it would become a habitat for thousands of organisms. It was a benefit which would not be enjoyed for many years.

The squid was not interested in the architecture of the ship nor the potential habitation it may provide. All it cared about was the sustenance it carried.

Behind the dull aroma of fuel was a scent of blood, emitting from somewhere within the ship. Entry was easy, for many breaches had been formed in its side. With no other organism daring to venture anywhere close, the cephalopod was free to lay claim to everything within.

Its leathery body, largely comprised of strong muscle tissue, scraped the edges of one of the entry points. Jetting water through its syphon, it moved through a large corridor.

Drifting in the space were the remains of multiple human occupants, floating about as though in zero gravity. Their bodies had been ravaged by some kind of violent circumstance before being crushed by the water pressure. Each one was coated in some kind of inorganic material.

Taking a moment to examine one of them, the squid quickly learned it could easily remove the garments. First, it was more interested in exploring a large chamber in the vessel's midsection, not far from the towering structure at its rear.

The chamber was larger than the corridors. Unlike their narrow designs, this area was wide and spacious. Inside, the creature found a myriad of dead organisms, all just waiting to be consumed. Many of them were trapped in their own tiny enclosures made of a similar, albeit weaker material as the ship itself.

Many different species met their end here. Some were primates, similar to the land-dwelling occupants who usually occupied these vessels. Others were aquatic, similar to the fish and cephalopods whom it shared the ocean with. There were many other dead creatures in this enclosure, none of which it cared to identify. All that mattered was they were edible.

The squid, capable of lifting over forty times its own body weight, made short work of the enclosures. It started with the primate corpse, its beak and tongue shredding the flesh until nothing remained but splintered bone and minced remnants of hair and meat particles.

Its digestive system went to work, quickly burning through the mass. After eating its fill, the squid settled in the chamber, guarding the remainder of its buffet. Several minutes passed, during which the creature experienced a strange sensation within itself. Many strange sensations, happening all at once, both pleasant and excruciating.

Pain coursed through its body. The beast failed to understand what was happening. It was not being attacked and it had not consumed any indigestible material to expel. Equipped with a highly advanced immune system, the beast rarely felt the strain of illness. Up until now, all ailments it experienced came from outside factors, namely predators and resilient prey. It did not know what was wrong, but was intelligent enough to make the connection between the symptoms and the recent meal.

Yet, it did not want to regurgitate. On the contrary, despite the pain coursing through its body, the beast was hungry again. Even after consuming over thirty percent of its body weight, it felt as though it had not eaten in weeks. With hunger and pain driving it to madness, it used its ten limbs to tear at the cages where the remaining animals were stored.

It stuffed its beak, loading itself with new flesh, oblivious to the serum which had corrupted their DNA—and was now altering its own.

CHAPTER 8

Shades of gold stretched from the horizon, initiating the arrival of dawn. In the hours since the helicopter exploded, the squad worked on reuniting. Having been dragged east for several hundred feet by the fish, it took a while for Serrano's group to locate Rymer and Kresmery.

The two men had taken refuge on a few floating steel plates, drifting several yards apart from each other. Serrano, Weston, and Jarman used their hands to slowly paddle their makeshift raft.

"You know, you could've just flipped the lifeboat over and rode in that," Rymer said. "Might be more efficient."

"The thought came to mind earlier," Jarman said. "Unfortunately, there's a crack in the hull. If we flipped it over, we'd just take on water."

"Wow," Rymer muttered. "*Nothing's* going right on this trip."

"What the hell happened over there?" Kresmery asked. "We could see the chopper's lights as it went down. Then we saw the explosion."

"Thank this guy," Jarman said, elbowing Dr. Nore. "Or rather, his pet fish."

Kresmery glared in disbelief. "That *shark* managed to take down the helicopter?! How?"

"It turns out it had a few tricks up its sleeve—fin. Whatever." Jarman waved his hand dismissively, not keen on revisiting the topic.

"It was able to detach some of its thorns and throw them at the Seahawk," Serrano explained. "Doesn't matter. It's dead now. We managed to detonate the rockets while the shark was near the crash. Boom. Dr. Nore can kiss his 'perfect specimen' goodbye."

All eyes turned to the scientist. He sat on the plywood sheet, hands tied behind his back, eyes down.

"Aww, is someone sad?" Kresmery said, pretending to wipe tears from his eyes. "You're lucky we didn't feed you to the thing."

Rymer shook his head and waved his hands, bordering on going insane. "Wait, wait, wait. Hold on. We're talking about the shark 'shooting thorns' as if that's a normal thing."

"You saw the animals in the lab," Jarman said. "Did anything in there strike you as normal?"

"No, but…" Rymer trailed off, unsure how to articulate his thoughts. "I guess it just seems impossible that such a creature could exist, even with genetic engineering. And what for? Is there a market demand for fucked-up sharks?"

Jarman chuckled. "Oh, it's fucked-up alright, thanks to me, Weston, and the Cap." He mimicked an explosion sound, elbow, making sure to be right in front of Dr. Nore when he did it.

"Okay, biologically fucked-up," Rymer said.

"Yes, yes, yes. We know what you mean," Jarman replied. He looked at Dr. Nore. "Well, Doc. Since we've got a few minutes, why don't you explain it to us."

"Your client didn't explain it to you?" Nore asked, not bothering to make eye contact with him. "Then again, I'm assuming you've been hired by the good ol' U.S. government. They're not necessarily known for providing the full picture."

"For once, we can agree on something," Weston said. "Go ahead, Doctor. Tell us why you were screwing around with those animals? Those things in the first cargo bay didn't look like they were enjoying themselves, and I don't think it was because they were locked in cages. I know pain when I see it. Even the fish specimens you had looked as though they were ready to smash their brains against the aquarium glass."

"Obviously, somebody was hoping to apply his research to military use," Kresmery said.

"Yeah?" Weston said. "So, is that the plan? Design an army of giant sharks for the Russians to use against the U.S. Navy?"

Nore chuckled at that. "That's quite a thought, isn't it?" None of the mercenaries shared the so-called lighthearted feeling. "No. I was using animals to test a special serum."

"Let me guess: you were planning to conduct human testing," Kresmery said. "Inject a bunch of soldiers with that shit and create a bunch of *Incredible Hulks*? Am I close?"

"Close enough," Nore said. "As you may have already figured out, the serum alters the DNA of its host, enhancing its biological structure."

"Those creatures didn't look enhanced to me," Jarman said. "Fucked up, maybe. Enhanced? Not really."

"Hence the term 'test subjects'," Nore spat at him. "That's the path of science. You keep getting it wrong until, finally, you get it right. And boy did I get it right. The October Trial was my first success. The shark is the prototype for what is to come. It endured a lot of pain in the process, but by God, it proved to be worth it."

Serrano shook his head. "Right. I'm sure that's exactly what the fish thought."

Nore turned his eyes to the mercenary leader. "What makes you think it didn't?"

"It's a *fish*." Serrano spoke through gritted teeth. It was the only way he could conceal the true extent of the pent-up anger billowing within him. "It's just an animal. It doesn't understand what you've done to it, and I doubt it appreciates it. This talk of worth and success comes from your mind and nowhere else."

"If you say so," Dr. Nore said. "Then again, it seemed to take great pleasure in going after your men." He smiled, deliberately trying to elicit a response.

"Just as it did going after yours," Rymer replied. He immediately realized his attempt to aggravate the scientist was futile. Those weren't *his* men, but his client's. Plus, Nore did not appear to be the type who gave a shit about most human life. The only thing he appeared even remotely emotionally attached to was his project.

"Indeed it did." Nore's tone confirmed Rymer's thoughts. "It's a hunter. My Titan Serum enlarged its body, as well as all of its internal organs. Including its brain. I'm not saying the shark is going to teach calculus, but compared to all other species of fish, it's a freaking genius."

"*Was*," Jarman corrected him.

Nore bit his lip, reflecting on the recent events. "Sure. Was. Go ahead and revel in the moment, soldier."

"Marine," Jarman corrected him again.

"Gun for hire," Nore replied. "Still cannon fodder for Uncle Sam. Just a little more expensive than before."

"That supposed to make me feel shameful?" Jarman said. "And, by the way, there's no such thing as an ex-marine."

Nore sniggered and watched the water. "But there is such a thing as a dead one."

A snarling Jarman passed his rifle to Weston and balled his fists. "That a challenge, Doc? Let me undo those restraints and we'll see who outlives the other."

"That's enough," Serrano said. "Jarman, zip your lips. You should know better than to let this asshole get inside your head. Don't forget, we killed the shark. He's just saving face."

"Dunno, Cap," Rymer said. He was staring at the doctor. "Doesn't look too heartbroken to me."

"Like I just said, he's saving face," Serrano said.

Even as he spoke, he could not help but study Dr. Nore's body language. Though he wouldn't admit it out loud, he agreed with Rymer's observation. When they first killed the shark, Nore appeared beaten down to a sensible degree. Enough so that Serrano was confident the guy had resigned himself to his fate. Now, just a couple of hours later, his sense of superiority was showing through the cracks.

The shark is dead. I watched it sink. He repeated that statement in his mind several times, assuring himself the fish was no more. It had to be dead. It wasn't moving.

The memory was pushed aside, making way for another one. For a moment, he was in Afghanistan, defending an outpost against some Taliban insurgents. He remembered multiple RPGs striking a tower, just a few meters from his location. The combined explosions had knocked him off his feet. For the next couple of minutes, he was a sitting duck. He remembered being awake at the time, staring up at the smoke-filled sky, yet being unable to move. He was left stunned. To this day, he thought of it as temporary paralysis. In almost every instance, it was brought on by a massive concussive force such as an explosion.

"Shit, I thought you were dead," one of his fellow soldiers said to him after Serrano had finally gotten off the ground.

He looked at the water, completely lost in thought.

It HAS to be dead. It hasn't attacked since the explosion.

It seemed like a rational thought. Wouldn't the creature want to make a grand return, especially if it relished in the misery it caused?

Serrano's mind went back to the battle at the outpost. He remembered needing several moments to get his wits back. If it was possible, he would have been more than happy to take himself out of the fight for a short while to pull himself together. Being the good soldier, he kept on fighting, but only because there was no other choice.

The shark, on the other hand, had the luxury of time. He had watched it sink motionless, but that didn't mean it didn't resume swimming after it disappeared from view.

He turned his eyes to Dr. Nore. No, the guy did not seem too broken-hearted anymore. If anything, it looked like he was trying to *appear* broken-hearted. It made Serrano think of a couple second-rate actors he had seen in a stage play at one point in his youth. After a while, those guys struggled to maintain their performances.

"So, what now, sir?" Weston asked.

Serrano gave one more look at the water. There was no point in speculating if the shark was dead. At this point, speculation was all it would be. There was nothing the team could do to make themselves more prepared than they were already. The only thing to do was figure out a way to escape.

"Well, I say we've done enough floating for one day," he said.

"Yeah, no shit," Jarman muttered.

"Do we have the SAT phone?" Kresmery asked. The somber looks on everyone's faces provided him with his answer. "Little had it, didn't he?"

"We don't have enough water to float here much longer," Rymer added. "In a couple of days, we'll be drying up like prunes in this sun. I suggest we figure out a new game plan."

"Already got one," Serrano said. "We have to find the Zodiac."

"The Zodiac?" Jarman said. He waved his hand at their surroundings. "Finding it in all this mess? For all we know, that thing's halfway to India by now."

"You have a better idea?" Serrano said.

Jarman exhaled through his nose, looked at the water lapping over the plywood, then shook his head.

Unfortunately, his point was still valid. Looking for that damn Zodiac in all of this wreckage was going to be a pain in the ass. Hopefully, it hadn't drifted too far away. Their lives depended on it.

He dug his binoculars from his vest and initiated the search.

Serrano did the same. With the glasses raised to his eyes, he combed the ocean for a black inflatable vessel… while also keeping an eye out for a dorsal fin.

CHAPTER 9

"Over there. I think I see something," Jarman said. He was aiming a pair of binoculars to the southeast. The rest of the team aimed their own glasses in that direction, catching the sight of a large black object in the distance.

It had been a long and exhausting search. Paddling their way through the accumulated debris was not an easy task. The mercenaries, all of whom had been through hell and back in countless occasions, were truly feeling the test of their physical endurance. Shoulders and arms ached. Their throats were dry, a misery exacerbated by the salty air. The sunlight, which they had longed for in the night hours, was now threatening to blister any exposed skin.

"You sure, Jarman?" Rymer said. "It's been over two hours. You've seen at least twenty somethings by now."

"Hey, I didn't blow up the ship," Jarman said. "Besides, what have you contributed lately to this survival effort? Aside from complaints, that is?"

"Hmm! I remember you scarfing down the protein bars I brought along just a few minutes ago," Rymer replied. "Doesn't look like the rest of you brought much."

"I brought this." Kresmery dug out a can of spam from a side pocket and held it high.

Rymer winced at the sight. "Spam?! What, are we in World War Two all of a sudden?"

"Ah, nice!" Weston muttered. "High sodium meal while we're hours away from dehydration."

Kresmery tucked the can back into his pocket. "Suit yourselves."

As the men traded verbal blows, Serrano studied the object. It was black and fairly large. With the sun assaulting his gaze, it was hard to confirm whether or not it was the Zodiac. Even hours after the sinking, there were still countless items drifting all around them. Some traveled far out to sea, making Serrano worry that their ride may have done the same.

"Quit squawking, ladies. Time to check it out."

"Hey!" Jarman feigned offense. "That's insensitive to refer to us that way. Women are capable too, you know."

"Prove it, then," Serrano replied. "Start paddling, *Jasmine*."

The other men laughed at Jarman's expense, then got to work. Using a few loose planks taken from the water, they steered their 'raft' southeast. A big, hulking mass, it resisted their effort. The wind threw a few small swells in their path, slowing them down even further.

Every few minutes, Serrano would take another look through his binoculars, hoping to identify the object. Not that it made much difference either way. At this point, they needed to search farther east anyway, having thoroughly checked west of where the *Griffin* had sank.

Muscles strained, the men grunting with each rowing motion. Thirst ravaged their throats, tempting each of them to drain the remainder of their canteens. Being good, disciplined warriors, they resisted. There were a few bottles stashed aboard the boat. Once they found it, then it would be time for a celebratory drink.

"Keep going," Serrano said.

"Nah, we thought we'd just sit here and work on our tan," Jarman remarked.

Serrano ignored the stupid joke, then gave a quick glance at their prisoner. Dr. Nore sat cross-legged on the center of the plywood sheet. In the time since they started searching for the Zodiac, he had hardly uttered a word. He, for one, hardly seemed concerned with their prospects of survival. If anything, he looked like a man who was simply running out the clock.

Serrano felt a sixth sense warning him that the doctor knew something he didn't. It was a feeling obtained after years of experience. The best and worst part about this special instinct was that it was almost always right.

Rifle stocks and metal shards plunged into the water and raked back, guiding the mercenaries ever closer to their salvation. After crossing several dozen yards, Serrano raised the glasses to his eyes once again. The other men did the same, each one equally desperate to see their Zodiac out there waiting for them.

"It's… it's a…" Rymer tried to stand up on the hull of the lifeboat, as if that would somehow improve his view.

Jarman lowered his binoculars and sat on his knees, defeated. "It's a cargo container." He resisted the temptation to throw the binoculars into the water in a fit of rage. "Son of a bitch."

"You've got to be kidding me," Kresmery said. He squinted through his own set of glasses, groaning as he identified the shape and textures of the rectangular object. "How the hell is that thing even floating?!"

"To fuck with us," Rymer replied. "That's the only reason."

"Probably the contents," Weston said. "It might be a refrigerated container."

"I wasn't looking for a literal answer," Kresmery exclaimed.

Weston shrugged. "You sounded curious."

"No, I'm pissed," Kresmery said. "We're floating miles from land. I can handle being in a pinch in a warzone. Getting shot or blown up—all parts of the job. Not drifting for eternity, dying of thirst, with only your spam to cheer me up."

"Hey, it could be worse," Weston remarked. "Jarman could attempt another magic trick."

"Okay, jackass." Jarman put his hand up and took a breath, preventing himself from going into an incensed rant. "Joke gets a little old after the hundredth time."

"Gentlemen, pull yourselves together," Serrano said. "We're not licked yet."

"Hey, he's calling us gentlemen instead of ladies," Jarman said. "That must mean he has confidence in us now." Nobody laughed at the attempt at humor. Jarman shrugged. "You know, I'll just go back to looking for the Zodiac. One of these times, I'll actually find it."

He raised his binoculars and scanned the southwest horizon, slowly turning southward.

"It's probably gone," Rymer said.

Jarman perked up, his gaze fixed to the south. "Uh, guys? There's a boat out there."

"Uh-huh," Weston muttered. "Coming from the guy who, less than an hour ago, managed to mistake a milk jug for the Zodiac."

"I had the light in my eyes," Jarman said. "Depth perception was off. Plus, my eyes are dry as shit. Secondly—there's a boat out there!"

Serrano aimed his binoculars to the south, then immediately lowered them. "It's a boat."

Now the other men were looking to the south.

"Hot damn," Rymer exclaimed.

It was a vessel which had seen plenty of use over the years. The paint on its bow, originally white, had chipped away and replaced with rust. An outrigger extended from each side, dragging a large net behind the vessel.

"Squid fishermen," Serrano said.

"At this point, they can be drug shippers for all I care," Jarman said. "Anything beats this hunk of literal junk." He put his boot on the plywood sheet.

Weston started waving his arms, sparking laughter from the others. He looked over his shoulder to sneer at them. "What?"

"They're half a mile away at least," Rymer said. "Not sure if they're gonna notice you from all the way over there."

"Alright, fine." Weston picked up his rifle and removed the suppressor. "Maybe they'll notice this." He pointed the gun in the air and put his finger on the trigger.

"Whoa, whoa, whoa!" Jarman moved over to him and forcefully lowered the rifle muzzle. "Not sure if random gunfire is the right way to go."

"Hate to agree with Jarman," Kresmery said. "But he's right. If they hear us popping off rounds, those guys are more likely to go the other direction. I know I would."

As they spoke, Serrano kept his eyes on the squid boat. It was moving due east, with no indication the crew took notice of the wreckage. If any debris had floated in their path, it went unseen. Before long, the boat would be completely out of sight.

"We need a flare," he said.

"I have a couple of flare sticks," Rymer said.

"Unless you're Hercules, there's no way you can throw the flare high enough for them to see it," Serrano replied. "We need a Very pistol."

Kresmery chuckled. "Sorry, boss, but I don't think we included one of those in our supply kit." His facial expression froze as he noticed everyone staring at the lifeboat he and Rymer were seated atop of. His next feeling was one of relief and humiliation. "Oh…right! I feel stupid."

"Should be a case with a Very pistol inside," Serrano said. "Congratulations, Kresmery. You get to dive in and retrieve it. Do it now, because we don't have a lot of time."

Kresmery looked at the waterline. The sliding door entrance was on the top side, meaning he would have to act fast, for the moment he entered, the ocean would come racing in.

He removed his vest and handed his weapons to the others, took a breath, then dove under the water. The lifeboat bobbed as he moved along its hull. A metallic echo reached Serrano's ears, meaning the merc had successfully opened the hatch.

A collection of noise followed as Kresmery searched inside the lifeboat. Seeing as the small, rigid-hulled boat was not properly deployed, all of its contents had likely been tossed from place. With the water rushing in, things were likely getting more chaotic and confusing for the mercenary inside.

With its inside flooding, the lifeboat gradually began to sink.

Rymer's eyes widened as he realized this. He quickly swung off the keel and carefully made his way over the sofa.

"Oh, shit, it's gonna sink," Jarman said.

Serrano cursed under his breath. He hoped that the lifeboat would remain buoyant enough to remain on the surface, but alas, the water weight was proving to be too much.

"Hurry it up, Kresmery!" he shouted.

The water steadily climbed up the keel, swallowing the vessel. With no sign of Kresmery, Serrano placed his rifle down and began removing his vest with intent to go after him.

Splash!

Kresmery popped out of the water, holding a two-foot case in both hands. "Got it!"

Rymer took the case, handed it off to Weston, then helped Kresmery out of the water. They removed the ropes connecting the lifeboat to the sofa, preventing themselves from being dragged under.

Weston wasted no time. He opened the case and removed the orange pistol. Stored with it were three flare cartridges. He loaded one into the weapon and pointed it high.

A squeeze of the trigger sent a blazing ball of fire soaring towards the blue sky. After four hundred feet, it began to arch back down to Earth.

Serrano watched the vessel. For the next minute or so, it continued on its intended trajectory, its large net in tow.

A horn echoed through the air. There was a sound of engines stalling, then starting back up. There was a faint reeling sound, which Serrano realized was a winch. They were bringing in their nets.

The boat turned to port and pointed its bow at them. He smiled. They had seen the flare.

"It worked."

The men high-fived each other. Kresmery and Rymer were quick to help themselves to their canteens. They were about to be rescued. The fishermen would have water to spare on the boat.

Jarman knelt by Dr. Nore. "Don't worry, Doc. Maybe we can cook you up some calamari before we haul your ass back home… What? You curious what time it is? Why you looking at your watch?"

Hearing that statement, Serrano looked at the doctor. He was angling his wrists to the right, trying to put his watch in view. Right then, there was a small ping from the device.

The former captain felt foolish. He didn't think anything of the watch. It appeared no different than any other ordinary smartwatch. If anything, he figured it was busted after being exposed to water. Even if it was able to put out a signal, it was hard to imagine getting one out in the middle of the ocean.

Serrano scanned the horizon. His first thought was somebody was tracking a signal from Nore's watch and was on approach. That would explain why the doctor seemed calm and confident this whole time. He looked in every direction, seeing nothing but the squid boat.

He focused his binocs on the vessel. It was a couple hundred yards away, its crewmen now in plain view. A couple of them were pointing at the mercs from the side deck and yelling in Somalian to the helmsman in the wheelhouse.

"What's the matter, Cap? Worried they'd turn out to be pirates?" Jarman remarked.

Dr. Nore's watch chimed again.

Serrano moved behind him and looked at the small screen. There was a tiny map image, with a blinking dot signaling the presence of something to the south. On the corner of the screen in tiny lettering were readings. Heart rate. Blood pressure. Depth.

CRASH!

"Holy Jesus!" Jarman exclaimed.

Serrano's eyes turned to the ship. As though struck by a tremendous uppercut, the fifty-foot vessel's bow lifted. Underneath its hull was a large, spiny mass.

The shark had returned.

"Are you kidding me?" Kresmery said. "It's still alive?"

For a moment, the boat appeared to teeter on its stern, ultimately crashing forward. The three crewmen were thrown into a panic. One of them pointed at the shark's position, his face and tone demonstrating the angst and confusion he was currently experiencing.

Propelled by a massive crescent-shaped tail, the shark circled its target. Its side-to-side motion increased, launching it at the starboard-side bow like a torpedo. Its pointed head punched through the hull. Shards of metal and fiberglass erupted from the impact. A second crashing sound immediately followed as the shark came out the portside, leaving a massive gash in its wake.

The ocean invaded the lower decks of the vessel, killing its engines within seconds. Up top, the captain and his three crewmen looked over the side, realizing too late that the vessel was about to make port on the ocean floor. Its bow dipped first, the rate of decline accelerating as more water filled the insides. Now, the stern had raised a few feet, only to slip into the water on a near-perfect thirty-degree slope.

Water rose over the gunnels and poured onto the deck, giving the newly-caught squid a fresh start at life. They swarmed the water, joined by the four crewmen. The captain, a man in his upper forties wearing a yellow ballcap, clung to the port outrigger while he attempted to get the raft inflated. His effort was cut short after he noticed a few swells coming in his direction.

He turned around and screamed as the pointed snout sprang from the water. The shark threw itself at its victim, closing its jaws over him and the outrigger. Fully committed to its attack, the fish did not slow down, but instead rammed through the arm of the vessel. With a deafening *SNAP*, the outrigger broke in two. Nearly impaling itself on the jagged spear-like end, the fish moved to the right, trailing blood from its gills.

Pieces of fisherman broke away as it munched on the boat captain. Without hesitation, it went after the next fisherman. Sadly, the man did not realize his frantic motions only served to pinpoint his location to the fish. It closed the distance and seized his upper body in its mouth. It shook him like a dog with its chew toy, ultimately severing him in half. His lower body, legs still kicking, were flung to the side, jetting blood from the waistline.

The two remaining fishermen went in separate directions, though not purposely. One of them slapped the water, paddling with all of his might. In spite of this, he was moving *backwards*. The ship completed its plunge, with the net drifting for a few extra seconds before following. The lines went taut and the nets went under, dragging down the unlucky fisherman whose foot was snagged. The fisherman made one final yell, reaching to the sky with arms fully outstretched. Coiled fingers slipped below the surface.

A few feet beyond them was the shark. It stopped to observe the man's predicament for a moment. Instead of going after the easy snack, it went for the final remaining crewmember.

As he watched it move in on the man, Serrano heard a low chuckle from Dr. Nore. The scientist wore his grin, watching his creation with admiration and pride.

"You enjoying this? Those men didn't do anything to you," Serrano said.

Nore smiled. "I am, as a matter of fact. In these last few hours, I've gotten to learn more about my specimen than in the years I spent experimenting on it."

Serrano didn't ask for him to elaborate, for he already understood. The fish had chosen not to kill the sinking fisherman. The man doomed to join his vessel on the ocean floor, making the kill complete from the fish's point of view.

Punctured by dozens of serrated teeth, the fourth fisherman convulsed in agony. A massive red cloud expanded from his position, carrying pieces of tissue and fabric. The shark vanished under the waves, but not before the mercenaries noticed its dorsal fin turn towards them.

"Oh, shit. It knows we're here," Jarman said.

"Everyone keep calm and keep your eyes peeled," Serrano said. He was on his feet now, weapon pointed at the water. Without saying a word, he scrambled to come up with a plan. Conflict was inevitable, and given the shark's durability, there was no way they were going to win.

Sweeping the weapon every which way, he watched for the dorsal fin to emerge.

Rymer let out a few shots to the east. Serrano pivoted, ready to join in.

"Aw, shit," the tattooed mercenary said. In the water was the writhing body of a six-foot blue shark who was inspecting a nearby floating object. After watching the poor animal suffer unnecessarily for a few moments, Rymer raised his gun to end its misery.

A splash of red water struck his face. The blue shark's misery had come to an end, albeit a more violent one than Rymer intended. In the blink of an eye, it was crushed and sliced in the jaws of the beast, who flung its body away before submerging.

Rymer and Kresmery struck its side with a few bursts. As usual, the bullets failed to pierce its skin.

"Thing's practically made of Kevlar," Kresmery said.

At this point, everyone was grouped on the plywood sheet, forming a circle around their prisoner. Each man took in slow steady breaths, keeping their heart rates from climbing too high.

The shark's dorsal fin grazed the sheet as it passed underneath.

Jarman pointed his gun westward. "There!" The fish had emerged on the other side of their position. Now at two dozen yards out, it started turning around to face them. Jarman tapped the trigger, stinging its flesh repeatedly. The fish jerked with each hit, but showed no signs of deterrence. If anything, it moved with increased intensity.

Weston fired too, striking it right on the nose. The shark raised its head and thrashed for a moment, lips peeling back to reveal blood-red gums.

Serrano joined the fray. With a tap of the trigger, he put a round through one of those triangular teeth, splintering it into multiple white shards. The fish jerked, the water exiting its right gill slits red with its own blood. The bullet, having entered its mouth, had pierced the softer flesh in the back of its throat.

Still, the shark did not slow or turn away. If anything, it moved with greater purpose.

Serrano clenched his teeth and awaited collision. Before he could shout to his men to brace for impact, he was jolted by a frantic Dr. Nore. The scientist had slipped his restraints under his feet to get his hands in front of him. He dropped to his knees and drove his hands under the water, frantically tapping a button on the edge of his watch.

A high-frequency sound coursed through the water.

Right then, the shark changed course. It went north, quickly putting several dozen yards between itself and its human opponents.

Dr. Nore exhaled, simultaneously relieved and frustrated. With a press of the same button, the soundwaves ceased.

"What the hell just happened?" Rymer said.

Jarman grabbed the doctor by the collar and yanked him to his feet before grabbing his wrist and shifting it high to reveal the watch.

"Got a secret toy, huh, Doctor?"

A devious smirk contorted Nore's face. "Had you boys been a little more thorough, you might've taken notice of my watch and confiscated it. I thought you were supposed to be the best of the best?" His smirk disappeared after Jarman forcefully yanked the watch from his wrist. It was tossed to Serrano, who quickly gave it a brief inspection.

Looking at the device, the Captain noted the icons on the small monitor and the labels on the buttons.

"The doctor has quietly been keeping tabs on his pet all this time," he said. "Looks like he's been monitoring its vitals. For such data to be wirelessly transmitted, the shark must have some kind of implant."

"What about the sound?" Weston said. "Sounds to me like that watch does more than check blood pressure."

Serrano knew Nore had no intention of providing that data. Not that it made much difference. Serrano was able to connect the dots on his own.

"The shark's attracted to low frequency signals and repelled by high frequency signals, specifically those emitted from this device. The implant probably amplifies the sound in the shark's brain. Otherwise, the sound would have to be on the same frequency as artillery blasts to drive the damn thing away. Am I close, Doctor?"

A look of admiration came over the doctor's face. "Well, goddamn. I guess you're a little smarter than I initially gave you credit for, Captain."

Serrano closed his eyes. The memory of the shark's attack during the attempted helicopter rescue replayed in his mind. In that moment he realized Nore had thwarted their plans for escape, drawing the shark in with low-frequency soundwaves specifically to take down the Seahawk.

"I ought to switch on the low frequency and make you swallow this damn thing," he growled.

"Before we do that..." Jarman was pointing to the northeast as he spoke. "I'd like to draw your attention this way for something which may lift your spirits..."

"Jarman," Kresmery spoke in a hiss. "If you claim you've spotted the Zodiac one more time, *you* will swallow that damn watch… Ow! Hey!" Jarman grabbed him by the ear and forced him to look northeast. Kresmery perked up, seeing the black speck in the distance. He raised his binoculars to his eyes, then swiftly turned to face Serrano. "Holy shit, even a broken clock… or Jarman… is right every so often."

Serrano aimed his own binoculars at the boat. Sure enough, it was there, drifting freely among other wreckage. It was between six and seven hundred feet from their position, gently drifting to the north. *Away* from them.

He panned the glasses left, catching a glimpse of the shark's dorsal fin to the northwest. It was swimming idly, possibly planning to make another assault.

"We can paddle over to it," Jarman said. "Might take a while, but since we have the watch, we can keep the shark at bay. What do you think, boss?"

Serrano looked at the watch and, pursing his lips, shook his head. "That would have been a good idea an hour ago." He faced the screen towards his men. In its lower right corner was a blinking bar. "Battery's running low. Even state of the art tech has limited battery life."

Weston dropped his hands to his sides. "We just can't win today, can we?"

"How much is left?" Rymer asked.

Serrano fumbled with the settings button, eventually accessing the battery life. "Eh, fifteen minutes."

"Great. Doc must've forgotten to plug it in," Rymer said.

"That, and the sound frequency probably takes a toll on the battery," Serrano added. "I estimate there's enough for one, maybe two sound bursts."

"We'll need more than that to paddle our asses all the way to the Zodiac," Weston said. "Even without the lifeboat weighing us down, this thing is a bitch to move. The shark will come at us nonstop."

"Wait, hang on. Let me see that," Jarman said, extending his hand. Serrano bitterly handed over the watch. Jarman pulled his own smartphone from his vest and removed the case.

"What are you doing, Jarman?" Serrano asked.

"Please don't say another magic trick," Rymer added.

Jarman stuck his tongue out at them. "Oh, ha-ha. As a matter of fact, yes, I am performing a magic trick. I learned this when I was dating this girl in Denver. She showed me how to get a charge without plugging anything in." The men snorted. Jarman bit his tongue and waited for the innuendos to come his way. "Okay, yes. I know how that sounded."

"How'd she do it?" Kresmery asked. "She make you watch?"

"While someone else came to service?" Rymer said with a laugh.

Even Serrano felt the need to join in.

"Considering his success rate on magic tricks…"

The team chuckled.

"Ah, yes. We're trapped in the middle of the ocean and being circled by a forty-foot spino-shark, but at least I can count on you assholes to zing me," Jarman said. "BACK TO MY POINT; there's a way to charge a smartphone or smartwatch using another smartphone. She showed me how. I'm trying to remember. Just give me a sec."

"Please tell me you were paying attention to the lesson and not her cleavage," Weston said.

"A pro can do both!" Jarman exclaimed.

Weston turned to Serrano. "Sir. We're doomed."

"Ye of little faith," Jarman said. "Just wait. I think I got it figured out. I can sync these two devices together and get some extra charge to this watch. They must be close together. Maybe not touching, but close."

"Kinda like you and that girl you were dating?" Rymer asked.

Jarman made a face, then returned to his task. Over the next couple of minutes, he made another face. An irritated one.

"Hang on, this thing is being a dick."

"Looks like you can't manage it," Kresmery said.

"No, I can get it…"

Another minute passed, during which the shark's fin was now moving toward them.

Weston swallowed. "Jarman?"

"Hold on."

The fish closed in within thirty feet.

Serrano snatched the watch from Jarman and plunged it under the water. He hit the high-frequency emitter. The watch let out a loud burst of sound equivalent to the speakers in a Deep Purple concert.

The shark turned around and fled west.

Weston relaxed and lowered his rifle. "Too close."

"How much time is left, Cap?" Kresmery asked.

Serrano looked at the watch. "Eleven minutes."

"I can get a charge," Jarman insisted.

"No, we don't have time. We're gonna have to make do with what we got," Serrano said. He put the watch on his wrist. "How many grenades do we have left? I have one."

The rest of the men checked their supplies.

"Two," Rymer said.

"Two," Kresmery added.

Jarman and Kresmery lifted their last remaining grenades, simultaneously replying, "One."

"Seven total," Serrano said. "It'll be hard to blow that fish up with these—it's fast as a rocket—but the acoustics ought to keep it at bay. And maybe you can time your throws just right to get the shark in the blast radius. The soundwaves and concussive force ought to drive it away."

"'You'?" Jarman said. "As in 'us'?" He pointed at himself and the other team members. "What are you going to do, Cap?"

Serrano looked to the inflatable. "You said it yourself, Jarman. It'll take too long to row this thing all the way over there. It'll be faster if someone swims out there."

"You're going to swim out there?" Weston exclaimed. "In the water? Where the fish is?"

"Last I checked, you don't swim *out* of the water," Serrano retorted. "This is our best shot. I'll use Nore's watch to keep the shark off my back. I'll get on the boat and come back for you. Then we hightail it out of here."

"With the shark in pursuit," Rymer said. He cleared his throat after receiving a sizzling glare from his commander. "But that beats floating out here for eternity."

Jarman shrugged. There was no point in arguing with Serrano. As usual, the guy was right, even if the odds were not in his favor.

"Your funeral, Cap."

Serrano rolled his eyes. "Fabulous. Good to have friends."

CHAPTER 10

From the tip of its tentacles to the fins on its mantle, every nerve in the giant squid's body was on fire. Its soft and flexible body twisted and pulsed. Its siphon jetted water uncontrollably, ejecting waste and blood. Its sense of awareness came and went as the hours dragged by. The cephalopod had no understanding of what was happening to it. It was intelligent enough to surmise that these physiological issues stemmed from the dead animals it had consumed in this metal chamber.

Its flesh shifted and contorted, as though being digested and transformed into something else. Its color took on a blood-red complexion. Its body gradually increased in mass, soon filling up most of the chamber. Its eight arms and two tentacles, originally covered with leathery skin, were now lined with bony spines, much like the hooks hidden within its suction cups. Even its beak grew; a process which proved to be the most excruciating.

Though it could not see, its mantle had taken on a new appearance. Its basic shape remained the same, albeit larger, but its flesh had grown hundreds of pores from which pointed spines extended from. Its flesh, while still flexible and unhindered by an internal skeleton, had grown a top rigid layer, resembling a thin version of the armored shells used by crustacean bottom dwellers.

When it was conscious, it experienced enhanced senses. Its eyes pierced the cloudy residue in the chamber, detecting every detail on the wall opposite itself. Every swirl of ocean current, every faint tap on the hull, and every movement was detected. It learned of faint everyday sounds it did not even know existed before today. The same occurred with its sense of smell. Every scent within a mile radius was detected by its enlarged brain. Urine, fuel, blood, flesh, sediment, metal—even the slime secreted by underwater invertebrates and some fish.

Despite the nonstop agony, the squid experienced pangs of hunger. Those pangs became a fire within its body. A discomfort far more agitating than the process of mutation, its only remedy was consumption of flesh. During its mutation, the squid continued feeding, unwittingly fueling its transformation all the more. Now, with its mantle over thirty feet long and its two main tentacles over a hundred feet, it needed to escape this prison.

Too large for the passageway, the creature exhibited another trait of its mutation: Strength. Its arms, lined with thick muscle, bent over the edges of the open doorway and pulled. The metal wall around the rectangular entry squealed and bent. With added force, it tore like paper. The squid continued tearing up the wall until it was wide enough for its mantle to pass through. The corridor was wider, making for a tight, but workable journey for the breach where it had initially entered the ship.

Now in the open ocean, it beheld the sights, smells, and sounds of many other organisms. When the vessel struck the ocean floor, the shockwave and the expelling of fuel had driven off everything. Now that the wreck had settled, the ocean's inhabitants were eager to investigate. Bony fish, sharks, and schools of cuttle fish circled the bow of the vessel, unaware of how the pollution would affect their health.

As it turned out, oil exposure was the least of their worries.

No sooner had the squid make eye contact with a pair of sharks did it lash out with its ten limbs. The two main tentacles seized their cigar-shaped bodies, constricting them like pythons and penetrating their skin with razor-sharp hooks. The unsuspecting creatures struggled within the tight grasps, the lassos tightening with each thrashing motion.

One after another, they were pulled to the squid's beak. The first was decapitated, the other held in place and scraped by the razor-lined tongue. A storm cloud of blood whirled around the motion, attracting a few other fish and sharks—all of whom were snatched by the eight tentacles and imploded in a colossal grip.

For the first time in its life, the squid killed for the sake of it. Sure, it fed on many of its victims, but even without the desire to feed, it bore an unquenchable impulse to kill. It was an undersea murderer. It spared nothing, nor did it discriminate. Everything around it deserved death as far as it was concerned.

The result was a killing spree. Animals, big and small, were eaten, crushed, or pulled apart. The odor of blood overpowered that of fuel. The sight of life had been replaced by that of vast death. Once again, the layout of the sea floor had been changed. This time, instead of impact, it was the embellishment by dozens of mutilated bodies. Many sounds echoed through the water, all of which were from frantic movements of fish and sharks fleeing the area.

Before long, the squid was alone. Though surrounded by the mutilated bodies of its victims, its newfound yearning to kill was yet to be satisfied. In fact, it only intensified.

The squid may as well have become an entirely different animal entirely, for both its mind and body had been drastically altered. No longer was it simply a squid.

It was a murderous savage whose size and power dwarfed most other animals in the sea.

A titan.

Boom!

From the ocean's surface came a new sound. The squid could not identify the source, but could detect the vibrations coursing all the way to the bottom. Such vibrations often stemmed from collision. Collision often indicated conflict.

Expelling water through its siphon, the creature ascended. Before long, it was embraced by the reach of the morning sunlight. The glow above outlined the shapes of numerous floating objects. Waiting sixty feet underwater, the squid heard two distinct types of sounds. One was distortion from a large object moving at intense speed somewhere to the west. The other sounds were thumping noises coming from a rectangular object drifting several dozen yards to the north.

Splash!

A third sound. A land-based organism had entered the water and was urgently swimming away from the rectangle. Immediately, the squid's urge to kill kicked in. It moved a few meters closer, then stopped. The large organism swimming west of the squid's location had turned. With a burst of speed, it was moving toward the human.

The advanced eyesight identified the shape of a forty-foot shark. Bypassing the rectangle, it sped toward the human, who swiftly stopped and turned to face the predator as though to fight.

A high-frequency soundwave surged through the water. Both fish and cephalopod were driven back, their brains overloaded with auditory sensation.

The squid descended twenty feet and held position. The urge to kill was intense, but it did not override its sense of self-preservation. Unlike the ocean floor, where the squid was unmatched in its ferocity, there was an element of danger up here. The sheer size of the shark alone was cause for concern. Then there was the unfamiliar element from the human. What that sound was, the squid did not know. Such instances required a visual survey before taking action.

It waited and observed. The shark was moving southwest toward the rectangle.

Boom! Boom!

Two concussive sounds forced it to retreat westward. Shockwaves swept over the tentacled observer below, who quickly drew a conclusion. Though it had no understanding of the exploding weapons, it was smart enough to know they came from humans. There were a few trapped aboard the wreckage and were in the process of fighting off the shark.

Alas, the squid devised a tactic. It would gladly slaughter the humans to satisfy its newfound bloodlust, but first it needed to rid the world of the only sizable competition in the area. Solely focused on the humans, the shark appeared to be blissfully ignorant of the squid's presence, granting it the element of surprise. It was an advantage the squid planned to utilize.

All it needed was for the right moment to present itself.

***

"Oh, Andrew, you dumb shit. What the hell were you thinking?" Captain Serrano mumbled to himself. As soon as he hit the water, he began second-guessing his game plan. He was essentially a sitting duck, with nothing but loud noise to defend him against the forty-foot monstrosity which cleaved the ocean's surface with its dorsal fin. The wristwatch was reading five percent now, enough for one more soundwave.

The Zodiac was maybe five hundred feet ahead of him. Drifting *away,* of course. It was one of those days where practically nothing went in his favor.

Maybe not entirely nothing. The plan was working so far. He had successfully repelled the shark with Dr. Nore's wristwatch once so far. When it turned its attention to the team, it was repelled by a pair of grenades. As of right now, it was somewhere to the west. Right before Serrano had hit the water, they had used a grenade to drive it away and give him a chance to make a head start. Having started with six, they now had three left. The seventh was in Serrano's possession. If the plan went sideways and he became shark food, he would make sure to go out with a literal bang.

Jarman was cheering the Captain on from the raft. "Let's go, boss. You've got this! Shark's nowhere near ya. Just keep swimming. Just keep swimming."

Serrano looked back. "If you sing that damn song, I'm leaving your ass behind."

Jarman gave him a half-hearted finger salute. "Okay, Mr. Grumpy Gills."

"Jesus…" Serrano continued on. He wasn't sure what was worse; being in the middle of the ocean with a mutant shark, or the fact that Jarman got that damn song stuck in his head.

He could finally begin to make out the details of the Zodiac. No longer was it a speck in the distance. He was maybe four hundred feet away now. He spat seawater and slowed his breathing. He was a good runner and climber, but swimming long distances was not his strong suit. Usually, he relied on diver propulsion vehicles and other equipment to get him through the water. Today, he was left with only his hands, feet, and stamina. If Blake was alive, Serrano would gladly have allowed him to make this swim instead. The guy was a natural swimmer. He could practically glide through the water as if he had fins. Even Little would have been pretty well suited for this task. Despite being a big guy, he was pretty spry in the water.

The rest of the team matched Serrano's abilities. Even now, with all of the second-guessing going on in his head, Serrano had no intention of letting any of them go in his place. The mission as intended was over. Now, the job was to keep his remaining team members alive.

After several more strokes, he stopped to gauge the distance between himself and the boat. It was closer, though it was still drifting north. If that wasn't enough to make this task all the more difficult, there was a heap of floating debris drifting in his path. A large container was nearby, still afloat, its doors having been opened during the sinking.

He glanced to his left in search of the dorsal fin. There was no sign of the fish, which was simultaneously relieving and worrisome all at once. As the moments passed, the latter feeling overpowered the former. No way did the fish vacate the area.

Serrano turned on his back, backstroking while looking at his team. "You guys see it anywhere?!"

"No. It went under!" Weston called back.

Serrano's pace naturally quickened. He gripped his grenade, turning his eyes every which way. The dorsal fin was nowhere to be seen.

"Wait a sec…" He dipped his head under the water—just to see those massive jaws part. Lips peeled back, revealing pink gums and triangular teeth. A burst of air bubbles exploded from Serrano's mouth, the word "Shit!" muffled by the ocean.

His hand went for the watch. With a press of a button, a deafening sound boomed from the speaker.

Those jaws clamped shut and the shark made a sharp turn, abandoning its target in favor of separating itself from the source of that unbearable high-frequency soundwave.

Serrano surfaced, drew a breath, and glanced at the watch. One percent remained.

"Go figure."

Maybe it was enough to get out one last small echo. He wouldn't know until the opportunity presented itself. For now, Serrano had no choice but to assume the device was useless.

Gunshots echoed from the makeshift raft. Jarman and Rymer were unloading into the fish.

BOOM!

A grenade discharged, resulting in a towering wave.

"I don't see it," Rymer shouted. "You think we got it?!"

"Nope!" Jarman said. He was pointing south. "There it is! Hurry it up, Captain! This thing's pissed!"

Pointing himself at his destination, Serrano kicked and pulled at the water with all of his might.

Two hundred feet to go.

One-fifty.

Just a few more seconds, and he would be seated at the helm.

Jarman tapped the trigger, striking the shark's nose repeatedly. "Come on! Die, you son of a bitch!"

Not only did the shark refuse to do so, but it was livelier than ever. Closing within thirty feet, it raised its head and revealed the inside of its throat, giving its prey a brief view of their fate.

"Here! Eat this!" Weston said. He armed a grenade and chucked it at the shark. The fish, as if it had predicted this tactic, made a fast dive. The grenade detonated where its open mouth had been two moments prior.

Mist fell around the bewildered team. Weston dropped his hands to his sides, staring wide-eyed at where his grenade had landed.

"Bastard shark knew what was coming," he said. "Bastard is smart."

Kresmery knelt at the edge of the sheet and peered into the water. "Your grenade landed pretty close to it. The concussion had to have shaken it up a little."

"We're talking about a shark that was in the close proximity of exploding hellfire missiles," Rymer said.

"Not that close," Kresmery replied.

"It knew to avoid the chopper's missile and it knew we were about to hit it with a grenade," Weston said. "The bastard is smart."

"I say we strap some explosives to Dr. Nore and toss him out there," Rymer said. "Then again, if only we had some more C-4."

Nore sat cross-legged, unfazed by the soldier's pathetic attempt at making a threat.

Jarman combed the water with his eyes in search of the fish. "It can't be that smart. The dumb shit keeps using the same pattern. If it was smart it would try a different strategy. Like attack from below or…" His voice trailed off as his mind replayed the image of the shark making a dive. He leaned over and looked straight down into the water below the sheet of plywood. Jarman turned around. "Brace for impact!"

Like a surface-to-air missile, the shark parted from the water, smashing through the wreckage in the process. The five men were flung from their sanctuary. Like meaty pieces of hail, they crashed into the water.

Jarman's body was completely vertical as he fell. Though it happened in the blink of an eye, it felt like slow motion for him. In that split-second, he witnessed Weston and Nore hit the water sixty feet to his left. Rymer and Kresmery were somewhere to his right. And directly ahead of him was the shark. It was airborne, now beginning its descent into the water. It landed at the same time as he did, only with more grace. As soon as it touched the water, its caudal fin went to work jetting it under the ocean.

Jarman, on the other hand, was jarred by the impact of his body flatly hitting the ocean's surface. The sting of saltwater assaulted his eyes. He tightened his throat, withstanding the natural temptation to inhale. Water swirled around him, pulling his rifle strap against his shoulder and neck. For a second, Jarman had the feeling that the ocean was intentionally trying to choke him out.

He exhaled, producing a stream of air bubbles, which immediately shot upward. Jarman, now knowing which way was up, followed them to the surface. He took a much-needed breath and got a visual of his surroundings.

Weston was thirty feet to the west, clinging to Dr. Nore with one hand while clutching a grenade in the other.

"Try one stupid move, Doctor, and I'll make you eat this," he said. Nore didn't argue. Like everyone else, he had his bell rung pretty good.

Jarman backstroked toward them, all the while searching for Rymer and Kresmery. The latter popped out of the water approximately one hundred feet to the east. By the looks of it, he had lost his rifle.

Jarman waved at him. "Hey! Kresmery! Over here!"

Kresmery made eye contact and began swimming for his teammates. "Where's—" He spat a mouthful of seawater. "Where's Rymer?"

Jarman scanned his surroundings. "I don't know. Rymer?! Where the hell are ya?!"

A spray of red water provided the answer. The shark breached several yards to the north. Its jaws were clamped shut, driving several teeth into Rymer's squirming body. The soldier opened his mouth to scream, but vomited blood instead. The teeth sank deeper, piercing his stomach and lungs.

Proudly displaying its victim, the shark moved west, watching the remaining humans with its left eye.

By now, the three mercenaries were shoulder-to-shoulder. Kresmery had found a floating cushion on his way over. It wasn't much, but it managed to keep them afloat for the moment.

"You motherfucker!" Jarman roared. He fought against his rifle sling as he tried positioning the weapon to fire at the shark.

Rymer let out one last gurgle. Bones cracked loudly as those jaws closed the rest of the way. His upper torso fell away, trailing intestines and bits of other organs.

"It's turning this way," Kresmery said.

"I know! I can see too!" Jarman responded.

"What are we gonna do?!"

"Shut up, will ya! Just shut up!" Jarman moved behind Dr. Nore and used his shoulder as a resting post for the barrel of his rifle. The shark was moving in their direction now, spewing bloody water from its gill slits.

The doctor tried moving out of the way, only for Jarman to strike the back of his head.

"Not so fast, Doc. If I'm gonna get eaten, so are you!"

With that said, he depressed the trigger. The magazine quickly emptied, each bullet proving as ineffective as the next.

The shark quickened its pace, jaws agape.

Serrano was just a few yards from the Zodiac when he heard the impact. Looking back, he witnessed the flipping of the wreckage, and a few moments later, the death of Rymer.

He had a millisecond to come to terms with a certain reality. There was no way he would be able to rescue his men in time. Even if he was aboard the Zodiac right now, the shark would ravage the team before he even got halfway there.

One idea came to mind. He looked at Dr. Nore's watch and the low-frequency emitter.

It's deterred by high frequency sound and attracted to low frequency sound.

Lacking any time to think his idea over, he pressed the button and prayed there was enough power to get a burst of sound out. Serrano could not hear anything. He gave another glance at the watch. The screen was now black, the power completely drained.

He slapped the water. "Damn it! God—" His tantrum ceased with the realization that the dorsal fin was now turning in his direction. Once again, he simultaneously was relieved and anxious.

The good news: the plan had worked. The shark was drawn away from his men. The bad news: it was now coming for *him!*

If Serrano were to write an autobiography on his life, he would call it Think Fast, for that precisely summed up his career. Today was the pinnacle of that sentiment. The shark was coming and he only had seconds to figure out what to do. Boarding the Zodiac would not do much good. The shark would plow right through the damn thing before he could start it up.

He looked to the floating container.

"Fuck it."

He swam with all of his might, not daring to look in the direction of the shark. The doors were just a few feet away.

"Captain! Look out!" Jarman shouted. "It's coming for you!"

"YEAH, NO SHIT!" the panicked Serrano shouted back, scooping fistfuls of water. "Why don't you tell me 'cows go moo' while you're at it?!"

"Hurry up! It's getting closer!"

Serrano was cursing with each frantic stroke at this point. "Shit! Shit! Shit! Shit!" The tip of his fingers touched one of the doors. He secured a grip, then dared to look in the direction of his pursuer. Just like before, he saw it right as it sped at him with open jaws. "SHIT!"

He swung the door open and put it between himself and the fish.

BAM!!!

The impact knocked Serrano backward. His shoulder struck the lefthand door, which prevented him from tumbling far out to sea. Righting himself, Serrano clawed at the water until he was in the mouth of the container.

Boots struck solid metal. Serrano was standing upright on the container floor. Right away, he fell to his knees as the container was vehemently shaken. Behind him, the shark was biting on the door it had crashed against. The hinges squealed and bent. A moment later, they broke away from the frame entirely. Biting with its jaws and slapping with its tail, the shark reduced the large rectangular piece of steel into a misshapen piece of scrap.

It turned its eyes to Serrano. The container was at a downward angle, kept afloat only by a few large buoyant items in the back.

Serrano propped himself on his heels and dove farther into the container, heaving himself over a pallet of furniture. The shark chased after him, driving its entire head through the entrance.

Jaws snapped, emitting a foul odor of saltwater, bile, and flesh. It raised its head, striking the ceiling, then brought its chin down on a pallet. Wood and furniture burst into small shards which zipped in all directions like grenade shrapnel.

One of them caught Serrano in the back, dropping him right after he had stood up.

"Son of a—" He pulled the thin sliver of wood from his flesh and spitefully tossed it at the fish.

The shark was out of water at this point. Like a massive inchworm, it tried wriggling its way closer to its prey.

Its weight tilted the container to a thirty-degree angle. Pallets, loaded with cargo, began to slide. Serrano had just stood up when he was hit in the back by the nearest one. The impact jostled him right to those snapping jaws.

He threw himself to the left, dodging a chomping motion. As a result, Serrano was trapped between the wall and the right side of the creature's head. The big black expressionless eye burrowed into him, the arching of the shark's neck indicating its intention.

Pallets converged near the opening. The pileup of product ravaged any hope for the commando to make a run for the rear of the container. At the same time, there was no chance of slipping past the shark. It was pressed firmly into the container, its girth taking up most of the space. Even with the supplies falling against its snout, the fish remained lodged, and its attention locked on its target.

The side of its snout struck Serrano, knocking him against the wall. Jaws clamped, the teeth grazing his pants. In a rowing motion, it brought its head to the left, knocking away some of the product. It was the equivalent of pulling a punch before striking. The fish whipped its snout to the side again, and again, Serrano was smacked against the wall.

His ears rang and his head throbbed. Additionally, his temper grew red hot.

"Alright! I've had enough of this shit!" He raised the grenade and pulled the pin. "You want a snack?! I'll give you one."

He waited for the opportunity to present itself. It wasn't long before those jaws parted again with intent to shut over him. The instant they did, Serrano let loose the lever and tossed the grenade into its mouth.

As soon as the metal ball touched its throat, the shark slammed its chin onto the floor. A rush of water swept into its open mouth and divided into individual currents which exited its gill slits. Unbeknownst to the fish, this natural course of events extended its life, for the grenade was swept out through one of its left gill slits and out into the ocean.

BOOM!!!

Hearing the location of the detonation, Serrano immediately understood what happened.

"Oh, you've GOT to be kidding me!"

His temper cooled, for the fish did not go entirely unscathed. The grenade, having detonated in close proximity, packed a powerful punch which left the shark stunned and flustered. More importantly, some of the shrapnel managed to pierce its hide, drawing a thin cloud of blood.

***

An opportunity presented itself. The tactic of waiting for a proper time to strike had paid off. The squid, watching with its enhanced vision, saw that the shark had wedged itself into the floating structure. Its caudal fin, swatting madly, indicated the creature was stuck.

Its body stiffened after the intense blast, suggesting the fish was injured or even on the brink of death. At the very least, it had sustained some sort of injury. The scent of fresh blood made its way to the squid, enticing it from the sanctuary of deep water and up to the fray on the ocean's surface.

Moving in a laser straight route, closing within two dozen yards, its eight arms and two tentacles uncoiled and sprang at the shark.

***

Serrano, taking advantage of the shark's lethargy, gave thought to cramming himself through a thin space between its neck and the container's opening. That thought was exiled once the shark 'awoke' with a resounding fury. It lifted its head high, denting the container ceiling. The jaws extended, not to bite, but in an intense expression of anger. As if to *roar*.

The Captain kept his back pressed to the wall, watching in fascination while the shark 'swam' backward into the ocean. He was no oceanologist, but he knew sharks lacked that particular ability.

With the shark gone, the container partially leveled out, allowing him to watch the fish continue its reverse motion.

"Oh, great. This thing can also… The hell is that?!"

He was still fascinated, but for an entirely different reason. The shark was not swimming, but was being *pulled* backwards. A horde of snake-like creatures had risen from the water and coiled around the shark. Having dragged the shark from the container, they sought to constrict its body until it was crushed into the size of a walnut.

Serrano studied the structure of those 'snakes', noticing two were longer than the others and had hooded tips, reminding him of a king cobra. Their rubbery flesh were lined with spines, the undersides equipped with circular objects. Suction cups.

It all came together. They were not individual serpents, but ten flexible arms belonging to one enormous beast.

"A fucking squid!"

The texture of its flesh, as well as its sheer size, indicated mutation. He did not recall seeing the animal amongst the lab experiments and there was nothing to indicate Nore had stored it in another section of the ship. Considering his grave concern for the shark's well-being, he likely would have expressed the same for the squid.

Only one possibility made complete sense. The creature was a regular member of the nearby ecosystem. When the *Griffin* went down, the cephalopod helped itself to the dead experiments, thinking them to be an easy snack. Consuming their screwed-up DNA resulted in its own biology rapidly altering. As a result, the squid was a shell of its former self. It was no longer a simple bottom dweller just trying to get by. It was a murdering fiend; A byproduct of Man's tampering with nature; A bloodthirsty mutant.

As much as Serrano despised the cause of the squid's current state, there was no denying the creature had arrived at a perfect time. For once, something was working in his favor. The shark was preoccupied, granting the mercenary a golden opportunity to board the Zodiac.

He would have to leave anyway. The container shifted forward, driven by the uneven weight of the product. The entrance dipped under the surface while an avalanche of furniture and wooden pallets resumed their slide, threatening to crush Serrano unless he moved.

He dove into the water and kicked his feet. Behind him, the container descended into a spin while vomiting wood and fabric. Some of them sank while others floated up behind him.

A strong current from straight ahead added to the chaos.

Serrano opened his eyes and took in a view of the two underwater titans. They were both submerged now, the shark struggling inside the grasp of those arms. Directly below it was the squid's mantle. It was completely vertical, the fins forming a perfect arrow which pointed downward. The eyes were black with a strange red circle around them, equivalent to the white of a human eye, except more demonic.

Its strength was demonstrated by its apparent calmness. The squid's body hardly seemed to fidget while its arms strangled the shark with an odd grace equivalent to that of a ceramic sculpture making a flowerpot.

On the contrary, the shark was nothing but motion, and for good reason. Serrano could see the indentation of its body where some of the tentacles squeezed. Its cartilage skeleton was being compressed on its internal organs. Its muscles were bruising, the stomach threatening to spew its contents, and the circulation likely being cut off from its caudal fin.

As it had tried with Serrano in the container, the shark turned its head in an attempt to bite one of the arms. They were out of reach, the shark lacking the flexibility to bend itself and secure a hold. The only range of motion was in its caudal fin. Its motion did little except move the shark forward, the squid dragging under it. All the while, the strangulation persisted.

Hooks dug into its flesh. The suction cups grinded against skin, the muscles working diligently to get those hooks deep.

One of them must have succeeded, for the shark shook with greater intensity.

It managed to rotate its body, aiming its right eye at its attacker. The squid appeared to stare back, unfazed by the hateful glare. Then again, it was ignorant of the shark's intention. As far as it was aware, the fish was simply a bigger version of its unmutated counterparts. It was not present for the demonstration of its ranged abilities which proved devastating enough to bring down a military helicopter.

The tail bent to the shark's left, then swung toward the squid. Three spines dislodged and soared through the water like high-caliber bullets. The first one missed entirely, the second grazed the back of the squid's mantle, the third struck it right below the left eye.

Pain rippled through the squid's body, momentarily loosening its grip. Several of those tentacles coiled back from the fish and grouped near the injury like royal guards protecting a king.

In one corkscrewing motion, the shark freed itself. Now, it had the range of motion to bite. It turned to its right and lunged at one of the arms. The jaws closed around the tough, leathery flesh. A purplish cloud jetted from the multiple incisions. The shark tugged, severing the arm from the squid's body.

Jetting water through its siphon, the cephalopod made distance, only for the shark to pursue.

Meanwhile, Serrano was lost in a trance, watching this horrible yet marvelous course of events. The aching of his lungs brought him back into reality. He shot for the surface, taking in a much-needed breath before getting a new visual on the Zodiac. It was a little over a hundred feet to the north, having drifted. Wide strokes and speedy kicking narrowed that distance.

His fingers touched the rubbery hull, a sensation he never appreciated as much as this very moment.

An eruption of water attracted his gaze. The two monsters had breached. The shark had a grip on another one of the squid's arms. Judging by the angle in which it was biting, Serrano believed it had attempted to go for the head, only for the squid to move at the last second. Nevertheless, the shark was still causing severe damage.

They barrel rolled over each other, the squid's remaining limbs attempting to pry the shark loose. With a wet, peeling sound, the two separated. The shark moved to the east, chomping on a second severed squid arm. Its opponent, trailing blood, turned around in pursuit of the fish. Despite its injuries, it had no intention of giving up the fight. Blood had been drawn. As far as either of these beasts were concerned, this ocean was not big enough for the two of them. Living to fight another day was only a privilege for the winner.

Serrano moved to the stern of the Zodiac and started pulling himself out of the water. Halfway out of the water, he gave a glance to the showdown. The two beasts had submerged, though the rippling of water near the container suggested their disagreement persisted down below.

He hoisted himself aboard, falling over the rubber gunnel onto the flooring.

"Finally."

He stood up and found Little's sniper rifle. Raising it to his eye, he used the scope to locate his surviving team members.

There they were, a little over eight hundred feet to the southwest. They were huddled together, looking in his direction. Either they were watching him, or the flamboyant activities taking place near his position.

A wall of water rose in front of the crosshairs. Serrano lowered the rifle, muttering a cascade of foul language as he witnessed the next stage of the fight. The shark was upright, its front half out of the water. The squid was in front of it, having wrapped its two main tentacles around its neck and body. The shark rocked left and right, jaws parted.

It fell backward, its pale belly exposed to the heavens. Its tail smacked the arms, pricking the muscular flesh with its spines.

For a few moments, the two creatures disappeared, only to resurface with double the ferocity. The shark struck the arms with its tail again, staking them with its spines.

The squid, appearing as though fed up with the shark, turned its body. Its powerful tentacles pulled the shark to the left—directly toward the container.

BAM!!!

The shark crashed against the corner with enough force to fold the thick metal onto itself. The forty-foot container rolled from the impact, losing a few more of its buoyant contents.

The shark corkscrewed until it slipped free of the tentacles. Failing to maintain their hold, they loosened up, then lassoed again, this time securing a new grip around its caudal fin.

Unable to move forward, the shark was trapped on the surface. The tentacles began pulling it back, the remaining arms dancing with the anticipation of grabbing ahold of their foe and ripping it apart. The beak was visible, its snapping motion expressing the squid's desire to taste shark flesh.

That desire paled in comparison to the shark's will to live. Giving up on temporary retreat, it angled its head and body straight downward. As if doing a cartwheel, it turned itself at a vertical angle. Its tail bent like the hammer to a revolver. Then, with incredible power, it sprung in a complete semi-circle. The squid, still clinging onto the fin, was thrown out of the water.

For the span of a moment, its entire maroon-colored body was airborne. Following the motion of the tail, it came crashing down—right onto the now-jagged corner of the container where it had thrown the shark moments ago.

Rocked by impact, the squid lost its grip. The shark freed itself and swam in a tight circle, ultimately aiming itself at its enemy's mantle. This time, it had an unobstructed shot at its target.

Teeth pierced the side of its mantle, their serrated edges sawing away and widening the incisions. The stunned cephalopod returned to life, its tentacles thrashing in the air like flickering fire until they were dragged below the waves.

Serrano started the engine, his ears welcoming the outboard's motoring sound. He engaged the throttle and sped for his friends.

Another wall of water reached for the sky, forcing Serrano to veer to starboard. The squid and shark reemerged, the former snagged in an organic trap jaw.

As Serrano sped past them, he got a glimpse of the bleeding mantle. The jaws were making short work of the squid's flesh. The tentacles had wrapped around the shark's tail and body, unsuccessfully trying to pull it from its mantle. The shark chomped, gushing another fountain of blood.

The two main tentacles went for the head and eyes, grazing them with their hooks.

This time, the shark released its grip, though only to redirect its attack. It whipped to the left and clamped its jaws on one of the tentacles, compressing the flesh and penetrating it with wedge-shaped teeth.

A brutal tug detached the limb from its owner. The squid jetted water through its siphon, attempting a retreat. The shark kept pace, grabbing the other tentacle. They disappeared under the water, then reemerged five seconds later. Locked in combat, the mutants rolled over each other, tentacles waving in madness.

The spongy sound of tearing flesh struck Serrano's ears. Having passed the creatures, he had to look over his shoulder to see the state of the fight. As he predicted, the squid's other tentacle had been severed and tossed aside. Having lost its main weapons, the cephalopod was left with nothing but six relatively short arms to defend itself with.

The shark made short work of one of those arms, tearing it away before circling around the remaining defenses. With a burst of speed, it closed its jaws onto the squid's rear fin.

Serrano turned his eyes to his teammates.

Jarman waved his rifle barrel, fearing the Captain could not see him. "Over here, boss."

Serrano brought the Zodiac alongside the men. He brought Kresmery up first.

"Sure glad you made it, sir."

Serrano chuckled. "Because you were concerned about me, right?"

"Eh…" Kresmery shrugged. "Sure. Let's go with that answer."

They shared a lighthearted laugh and pulled the remaining castaways aboard. Jarman was quick to pick up Little's sniper rifle and aim it at the brawl taking place six hundred feet away.

"The hell is that thing?!"

"A squid," Serrano said.

"Where'd it come from?" Weston said. "Was it aboard the boat?"

"Don't think so. I suspect it snacked on the lab subjects," Serrano replied. He gave the fight one final glance. The shark had a firm grip on the squid. The battle was moments away from its conclusion. "We won't have much of a head start. Weston, keep your Christmas trained on the doctor. The rest of you, keep an eye out for the fish. It's probably gonna be on our asses in a minute."

Weston drew his .38 and kept it pointed at Nore. "Better hope we survive this, Doctor."

Nore leaned back, appearing to be looking at the western horizon, completely uninterested in anything the mercenaries had to say.

Serrano gunned the engine, the propellor blades jetting water as the Zodiac shot westward.

***

From the tip of its tentacles to the fins on its mantle, every nerve in the giant squid's body was on fire. Its soft and flexible body twisted and pulsed. Its siphon jetted water uncontrollably, ejecting waste and blood.

Its flesh shifted and contorted, transformed into something much different than what it was minutes prior. Its blood-red complexion began to pale as its bodily fluids leaked through its many wounds. Its five arms refused the signals sent by its brain. Their appearance matched the soggy, limp postures of the severed tentacles drifting nearby. The nerves and muscles had shut down, rendering the arms useless, and the squid defenseless.

Though it could not see, its mantle had taken on a new appearance. The nerves in its body were on fire, alerting its brain to every millimeter of tearing flesh.

Its sense of smell remained active, taking in the odors of its demise. Waste, blood, ink, slime, as well as the familiar smells of creatures it had killed on the ocean floor registered in its brain. The presence of such a smell led the squid to a terrible reality. Its stomach contents had been exposed, meaning its mantle had been thoroughly shredded.

This realization led to a second one: the squid had been defeated.

The blackness of death solidified that fact.

The shark tore at the mantle and arms until there was nothing left to identify its opponent as anything but an asteroid field of soggy flesh and guts. It swam through the organic debris field, consuming a few bites while searching for any sizable remains to shred.

Its opponent was dead. Annihilated.

A sense of satisfaction warmed the shark's cruel mind, only to be cast aside in favor of the desire to resume its onslaught. A whirring vibration passed through the ocean, drawing the shark's attention to the west.

The humans had found a small watercraft and were speeding away. Casting aside its feeling of triumph, the shark raced after them. As a drug addict continuously tried to reach that first high, the fish needed to kill again.

Only one death could ever fully quench that desire.

CHAPTER 11

The debris field was far behind them now. The horizon was nothing but blue sky and water. Each man embraced the rushing of wind in his hair. After their previous situation, there was a new appreciation to be had for the simple things in life.

It was a luxury which only lasted a few minutes.

"It's on our six!" Jarman said.

Serrano turned to look. Sure enough, the dorsal fin was a hundred meters behind the Zodiac and gradually closing in. The debris field was now three miles behind them and there was nothing but ocean up ahead. He turned his eyes forward in hopes of finding some kind of sanctuary in the distance. Anything. A large boat—preferably a Navy ship. An island. Anything to get away from Dr. Nore's bastardization of nature.

So far, all he could see was blue.

Jarman was already putting himself in firing position with the sniper rifle. In the meantime, Serrano could do nothing but keep the boat moving forward.

"How the hell is it keeping up with us?" Weston said. "We're speeding at fifty miles per hour."

"It's strong and agile, but it's gotta tire out at some point," Jarman said.

"It just tore apart that squid," Kresmery said. "Doesn't the thing ever get full?"

"I don't think it's concerned about eating," Weston replied. "You've seen how effed up its outer body is, thanks to the experimentation. Just imagine how its brain looks. If you ask me, I'd say the thing is the equivalent of a madman. Only, it's a mad shark."

"A psycho shark," Jarman added.

"It's more than that," Dr. Nore said, sporting a devious smile. "It's a weapon."

Jarman tapped the frame of Little's sniper rifle. "No. *This* is a weapon. That thing out there is just an overgrown sardine with a little lab enhancement from you. A weapon is something you can aim, direct… *control.* You can't control that thing. Nor will you be able to control any moron human subjects dumb enough to let you inject them with your special serum. At best, all you'll end up with are an army of *Incredible Hulk* knockoffs whose sole focus will be to kill anything within reach. They won't listen to you. No more than that big fish will, I can promise you that."

"You think I cannot control it?" Dr. Nore pointed at his watch on Serrano's wrist. "I beg to differ. The specimen could have killed us right away if it wanted to. And believe me, it did want to. But there's a reason we're still alive. At least, why *I'm* still alive. You gentlemen just happened to have the good fortune of being close by. Regardless, it is because I've learned how to control it."

Serrano shot the doctor a bitter glance. "Maybe a highly educated intellectual like yourself won't care to hear the opinion of a simple gun-for-hire, but the high and low frequency soundwaves? Deterring and attracting the shark? All of that is manipulation, not control. Those are two very different things. Because, I'm not sure if you're aware of this fact, but if your experiment catches up to us, it's not going to kill just my team and I. It's going to kill *you*. Unless you have another special watch, you're nothing but an item on the menu to that thing."

Dr. Nore looked past the Captain at the blue horizon in their path. He did not appear to have any response, though he did not look like a man who had been outwitted. Like Serrano had suggested, he was a highly educated intellectual who did not care to hear the opinion of a simple gun-for-hire.

"It's getting closer," Jarman said. "Two-hundred-seventy meters."

Kresmery paled. "Son of a bitch is actually faster than the boat."

"Yeah, but even a mutant fish has got to tire out at some point," Serrano relied. "Jarman, demoralize the fucker."

Jarman placed the crosshairs to where the shark's face was likely to be in the following moment. He adjusted for the wind and the motion of the boat, and squeezed the trigger.

The shark jerked, generating a huge splash. Large swells rolled behind its caudal fin.

Jarman gauged its distance through the scope. "Son of a bitch. It's still coming."

He struck it with another bullet, producing the same agitated result. The fish was undeterred. Jarman shot it twice more. After the fourth hit, the shark jerked to the side and submerged.

Jarman swept the surrounding area with his crosshairs. The waves began to settle, leaving no indication of where the creature had gone to. If there was any certainty, it was the fact the thing was still alive.

"It's gone under."

"Is it still after us?" Kresmery asked, cupping a hand over his eyes to block out the sun.

"How do you expect me to know?" Jarman replied. He combed the area with his crosshairs, seeing nothing but ocean. "Either it quit or it's continuing the chase underwater."

"Makes sense," Weston said. "It's not stupid. It's not going to continue chasing us on the surface and get pelted by sniper rounds all day long. Hopefully it's smart enough to know there's easier prey out there. What do you think, Cap?"

Serrano tightened his grip on the helm. Whether the fish was chasing them or not, his plan would still be the same.

"I think we'll keep moving west," he said. "When we get a chance, we'll call our client and get a couple of Navy choppers out here and blast the thing out of the water. Thanks to Dr. Nore's tracker, they shouldn't have a hard time finding it. Isn't that right, Doctor?"

"Hmpf!"

Serrano glanced at Nore. He was staring forty degrees off the starboard bow. Serrano followed his gaze, spotting a black speck on the horizon. The Captain found a set of binoculars and placed them over his eyes. The object was still too far away for him to get a good look, but considering this was the ocean, there were not many possibilities as to what this 'speck' was beyond the obvious.

"What is it?" Jarman asked.

Serrano passed the glasses to him. "Looks like we've found a boat."

"That right?" Kresmery said. He moved to the starboard bow for a better look. "Can barely see it. You sure it's a boat?"

"Nah, it's a Starbucks," Jarman said. "Of course, it's a damn boat."

In the next few moments, they were able to distinguish the basic shape of the distant vessel. It was a fishing trawler, likely probing for mackerel, sardines, or anchovies. The helmsman had cut the wheel to starboard, pointing the bow southwards.

"It's a decent sized boat," Kresmery said. "Seventy… no, eighty feet long."

"What difference does it make?" Jarman said. "What? You want us to stop by and say hello? No thanks. This Zodiac can move twice as fast and has enough fuel to get us to the mainland. Stopping would only give the fish an opportunity to catch up with us. Assuming it hasn't given up."

"Doesn't mean the people aboard the trawler won't be in danger. Who knows? The shark might abandon us and attack them instead."

It was Nore who made the statement. The four mercenaries hit the doctor with inquisitive looks. Each of them shared the same thought. No way was Dr. Nore genuinely concerned for the lives of the fishermen aboard that vessel. Compassion was not his strong suit.

Serrano turned his eyes back toward the trawler. It appeared to be moving at top speed, right in their path.

"Jarman, can you get a visual of the personnel on that boat?"

The marine raised the binoculars to his eyes and zoomed in to the max. "Hmm. I've got three, no, make that four crewmen on the aft deck. There has to be at least one in the pilothouse. If we say there's one or two more in the galley, then altogether, I'd say six or seven guys. Sounds about right for a boat that size."

"Do they look like they're from the region?" Serrano asked.

Suddenly, it clicked in Jarman's mind what Serrano was inferring. At this point, the trawler was seven hundred meters to their one o'clock, still moving south. He gave the crew another good look.

"They don't look like they're from the Horn," he said. "Dare I say, they kind of look Russian."

Serrano veered the Zodiac to port. "Exactly what I was afraid of."

The crew aboard the trawler were moving across the deck with haste. They were aware their cover was blown. These were not fishermen devoting time to their livelihoods, but armed Russian mercenaries responding to a distress call set out by the *Griffin's* crew before it went under.

Unfortunately for them, their vessel had a max speed of twelve knots, a mere fraction of the Zodiac's.

"Ah-ha!" Jarman said, still studying the vessel through his binoculars. "I see some AK-74s."

The crew were not even bothering to keep up with appearances now. The trawler swung completely around, its bow now pointing southwest. As it did, Serrano sped the inflatable past it, keeping a distance of a few hundred feet.

With an obnoxious smile on his face, Kresmery held up a middle finger to the crew.

"Stupid sons of bitches. Look at that. They're still trying to follow us. As if they have any chance of catching up."

Weston and Jarman chuckled at that.

Serrano, however, did not. It was true the Russians were following them. What was the point if they had no hope of catching up? Desperation? Or was there a larger plan at play?

Right as that possibility entered Serrano's mind, he watched the horizon in search of other boats. So far, there was nobody else on the water.

The sky, however, was a different story.

"Captain?!" a worried Weston called out. He was looking to the south, eyes aimed upward. "We've got a new problem."

Serrano saw it. Moving in at nearly two hundred miles-per-hour was a Ka-60 "Kasatka" helicopter. It was painted green to give it more of an Army appearance, possibly to trick civilians into believing it was a local military aircraft. Serrano knew better.

In a few short moments, the Kasatka was no longer a tiny speck in the sky. It was now less than fifty feet above them, keeping pace with the Zodiac roughly seventy feet from its portside.

The starboard fuselage door opened, revealing two Russian mercenaries. One had a pair of binoculars in hand. He kept the glasses fixed on the Zodiac for a few moments before shouting something to his fellow crewman. Serrano could not hear what was being said, but he knew the body language. They were confirming Dr. Nore was aboard the vessel.

Jarman got into firing position and put the tail rotors in his crosshairs. Sensing the danger, the chopper pilot banked, sweeping over the Zodiac until it was traveling along the starboard side. Its portside fuselage door opened. The second crewmember knelt at its edge. In his hand was a six-cylinder grenade launcher.

Jarman turned to adjust. He put the chopper in his sights and began to squeeze the trigger.

BOOM!

A wall of water sprayed in front of him. A shockwave jerked the Zodiac to port, throwing his aim off.

The gunner fired again. The grenade struck down twenty feet ahead of the Zodiac, its explosion producing a small tsunami which engulfed the small vessel.

Seawater assaulted Serrano's senses. He cursed through clenched teeth as he fought to steady the boat. The Russian was deliberately missing. His goal was not to explode the Zodiac, but to topple it and rescue the special contractor.

A third shot was fired. This time, it hit behind the stern.

The grinding sound of engine mechanics and the stench of burnt fuel and metal alerted Serrano to the fact the motor was damaged. The inflatable went from fifty-miles-per-hour to nearly a dead stop.

Three more grenades were fired in quick succession.

BOOM! BOOM! BOOM!

Three bursts of flame and water erupted near the starboard bow. The shockwave flipped the Zodiac. The four mercenaries and their captive were tossed into the water, skipping like flat stones on a calm lake's surface before submerging.

Serrano was upside down when his wits returned. Surrounding him were shredded bits from the Zodiac's ravaged hull. He righted himself and shot for the surface. To his surprise, he had sunk several feet in the few moments he was in the water.

He stopped, finding a stiff Jarman descending to the depths. He was unconscious and being dragged to the depths by his gear. Serrano kicked his feet and went after him.

The water darkened the deeper they went. Before long, Jarman was starting to blend in with the black background that was the abyss. Not one to leave anyone behind, Serrano put all of his energy into his legs. Little by little, he closed in on Jarman. He stretched his arms out and bent his fingers, securing a grip on the shoulder straps on Jarman's harness.

Up they went, the marine waking up mid-ascent. Air bubbles spat from his mouth, the distorted words "What the fuck?!" managing to reach the Captain's ears.

Serrano slapped Jarman's face, snapping him out of his brief episode of panic. Having regained his focus, Jarman swam for the light.

Both men broke the surface.

"Where are the others?" Jarman asked.

It was a struggle for Serrano to search. Having already swum a great distance less than ten minutes earlier, it was a strain just to stay afloat. Realizing this, Jarman grabbed him by the arm and directed him north.

"There!"

Up ahead were the remains of the Zodiac. It was upside down, its hull completely collapsed, forming a pool of black rubber which drifted like a giant lily pad. The two men swam for it and secured a grip.

Able to catch his breath, Serrano assessed his surroundings.

The trawler was quickly approaching their position. The helicopter was hovering thirty feet above the water roughly twenty yards to his four o'clock. The crewmen were leaning over the side, watching something directly below them.

That something turned out to be a some*one.* Dr. Nore gleefully slipped on an inflatable donut they had tossed to him and waited for his pickup to arrive. There was the sound of frantic yelling inside, and all of a sudden, the chopper ascended. Nore was pointing to the east, yelling "Aim left. Aim left!"

The guy with the grenade launcher fired a couple of shots into the ocean, sparking a pair of explosions. From what Serrano could see, neither of his men were in that area.

It wasn't hard to piece together the facts. They weren't shooting to kill, but to deter.

Confirming that theory was the presence of a large dorsal fin. It shot to the north, away from the locations of those blasts. The shark had caught up with them.

It slowed its speed and began to circle back towards the doctor. Midway through its turn, it changed direction, having detected something that piqued its interest even more.

Serrano and Jarman turned their eyes to the shark's trajected path, finding a dumbfounded Kresmery thrashing in the water. He saw the fin and knew his ticket was about to be punched.

"Oh, you fucking shark!" Kresmery raised his pistol in one hand and a knife in the other. A true warrior, he chose to accept his fate. "Bring it!"

He let loose all fifteen rounds in his sidearm. The shark closed in as the final bullet struck its nose. Kresmery yelled in a combination of rage and pain as man and fish collided. He stabbed and slashed, breaking the knife on its hard flesh. Meanwhile, the wedge-shaped blades lining those jaws had no trouble mincing his meat. A fountain of blood gushed from the thrashing waves.

For Serrano, the only thing more enraging than witnessing the death of his team member was hearing the maniacal laughter from Dr. Nore and the helicopter crew. The doctor saw them and pointed.

"Looks like he's in the mood for more! Ha! Ha!"

Serrano watched the dorsal fin angle toward him and Jarman. The marine unslung the sniper rifle and rested the barrel over the Zodiac wreckage.

"Maybe I can catch him as he opens wide," he said in a snarling voice.

Serrano's attention was back on the chopper. He watched as it hovered over Nore, held up by spinning rotor blades which created the illusion of a constant circle.

"Give me that!" He snatched the rifle from Jarman and spun around to face the chopper. Steadying himself against the Zodiac, he took aim at the rotor mast. "Let's see how funny you assholes find this."

He squeezed the trigger.

There was a *PANG* of lead striking metal. Serrano hit it a second and third time. Smoke spewed from the top of the helicopter. The crewmen's laughter transformed into shrieks of horror as the aircraft banked heavily to port. It descended into a tailspin, sweeping over Serrano and Jarman before crashing several yards north of their position.

Rotor blades snapped as soon as they touched the ocean, resulting in a horizontal shower of metal fragments. Serrano and Jarman ducked under the water until the bombardment ceased. When they reemerged, they saw the chopper floating on its side. The hull was crumpled, the windshield had shattered, and the tail was on the verge of completely detaching from the body.

Jarman cocked a smile. "Nice shooting, boss."

Serrano tossed the weapon aside. Its magazine had run dry and the rest of the ammo had sunk to the bottom of the sea.

The crash had done more than satisfy Serrano's ego. The shark had gone under, its agenda of attacking the mercenaries momentarily thwarted by nearly getting smashed by five-thousand pounds of steel.

The trawler was just a couple hundred feet away and closing fast. Men with rifles gathered at the guardrail and took aim at Serrano and Jarman. The leader of the bunch shouted in Russian. Serrano knew the words and tone. The men were being instructed to open fire.

"Ah-ah-ah!!!"

That was not a Russian voice, but an American one. Serrano and Jarman turned their eyes to the doctor, just in time to see Weston sneak up on him. The angry mercenary put the scientist in a headlock and clung tight. With his revolver pressed to Nore's temple, he successfully got the crew's attention.

"You pull those triggers and I'll see to it your business goes belly up!" he shouted.

The Russian leader raised a hand and shouted a command to his men, ceasing the attack before it could begin.

Before the standoff could persist, a series of screams echoed from the helicopter wreckage. The chopper rolled on the water, pushed by a forty-foot mass that was desperate to get to the treats inside. It was rewarded for its efforts with the taste of one of the crewmen, who squealed as those jaws rammed multiple teeth into his body.

The fish shook its victim, flinging body parts without care. It swallowed the trunk and dug its snout into the chopper, quickly seizing the second crewman. A repeat of the same events took place, with the crewman vomiting blood as he was simultaneously impaled and crushed.

Serrano and Jarman joined up with Weston. The boat pulled up alongside them, the crew keeping their weapons trained.

"Speak English?" Serrano yelled to them.

"Let Dr. Nore go!" the Russian leader said.

"You have two options," Serrano said. "You can let all of us, including the doctor, become shark chow. *Or,* you bring all of us aboard. I suggest you choose quickly."

The shark circled the wreckage, leaving a trail of floating body parts in its wake. After a few passes, it moved in on the cockpit, eager to grab ahold of the pilot. After failing to get its head through the windshield frame, it grabbed ahold of one of the landing struts and dragged the entire aircraft underwater.

It wasn't long before the pilot was forced to abandon his refuge and swim for the surface. He emerged and drew a breath. That very breath was forced out of him, for the shark slammed its jaws shut over his midsection. A grinding crunch sound signified the splitting of his body.

The Russian crew leader barked orders to his men, who promptly tossed a pair of lifelines to the castaways.

Serrano unholstered his pistol and held it tight. A standoff was inevitable.

CHAPTER 12

"Get back! All of you, or the doc gets it!"

Serrano kept Weston in his peripheral vision, making sure he was ready to make do on the Captain's threat. Weston maintained his grip on Nore as they were hoisted onto the main deck. With sidearms in hand, the three mercenaries stood near their hostage, their backs inches from the gunwale.

On the main deck ahead of them were seven armed crewmen, with the boat captain standing on the flying deck on the structure. Behind them was a churning sea, where an angry mutant searched for more victims. Having found none, it took an interest in the trawler. It swam alongside the keel, grazing the hull with its spiny skin. Reaching the bow, it turned left and continued circling the vessel.

The tapping of its caudal fin against the bow resulted in a minor tremor that rippled underneath everyone's feet.

Nore was calm and still, hardly bothered by the prodding of Weston's revolver against his temple.

"So, what's the endgame, Captain?" he said. "Do you plan to continue this standoff until Doomsday? Or are we going to kill each other in a shootout?"

Serrano kept his eyes, and gun, on the crew as he gave his response.

"If triggers are pulled, you will be one of the first to die. Your employer—or his employers, for that matter—are not willing to let that happen."

The ship captain crossed his arms over the guardrail overlooking the main deck. Though dressed in average maritime attire, he had the presence of a career military man. The sight of a spectacular helicopter crash and the inevitability of a shootout hardly seemed to bother him one bit.

"Don't speak as if you have control over the situation, American, because you don't."

"No more than you do," Jarman barked.

Serrano studied the man on the flying deck. Slowly but truly, he came to understand that this was not any ordinary gun-for-hire, but the head of the operation.

"Let me guess. Comrade Baranov, is it?"

The man on the flying deck smiled. "If you know who I am, then surely you know of my reputation. My face is the last many have seen. Keep that in mind while we continue this conversation."

"Yadda-yadda," Serrano grumbled. "You're just another puppet who talks a big game. I know who really pulls your strings."

"You try to insult me by stating the obvious fact that I work for someone?" Baranov made a haughty laugh. "That's rich coming from a mercenary."

"Give it up, Serrano," Nore said. "You can still spare your friends."

"Right," Weston said. "I *totally* believe you guys are willing to chalk all of this up to one big misunderstanding and let us go."

"I was hoping to do more than that," Nore said. "My experiment may have eradicated your team. But aside from that, you all have proven yourselves to be men of extraordinary skill. And clearly, you're willing to work for the highest bidder."

Jarman scoffed. "Wait a sec. It sounds like you're trying to offer us a job there, Doctor."

"I doubt the Comrade will be on board with that," Serrano said.

"Yes, we have lost several personnel thanks to you," Nore replied. "That doesn't mean we can't stand to gain something from this unfortunate circumstance. You see, even with the breakthroughs we've enjoyed up till now, there's still a lot of work to be done before Comrade Baranov has his army. Until that time comes, and even after, there will still be jobs in which a trigger has to be pulled. A job for men like you. You've already demonstrated an ability to successfully go up against superior numbers, as well as being able to infiltrate enemy fortresses unseen. Sure, we can kill you now, but all that'll do is give the green light to the next band of gunslingers sent by the good ol' U.S. of A's government, thirsting to steal my expertise and data. They had their chance. They blew it."

"Now, *you* have a chance," Baranov added. "I'd suggest you don't pass it up."

Silence came over the deck.

Serrano, Jarman, and Weston exchanged glances. Each of them was in shock that Dr. Nore was actually making this offer. Behind that shock was the suspicion that it may be a ploy to get them to drop their guard. It made enough sense. Release Dr. Nore, their only leverage, only to take a volley of bullets two seconds later. Then again, everything he was saying made complete sense. An operation like this would certainly need men of Serrano's expertise. In some cases, the heads of such organizations were willing to overlook the damage caused by players for the opposing team if it meant a greater gain.

He gave thought to the team's predicament. Given the situation at hand, there was no chance he and his team members would be able to outshoot all eight Russians aboard this vessel. They were all armed with automatic weapons whilst the three mercenaries were down to handguns. It would take the speed of a comic book superhero to gun down all eight targets before they were torn apart by return fire.

"I'll give you a count of five," Baranov said.

"And then what?" Weston asked.

"Then we assume you're declining the offer and we'll start shooting," Baranov answered.

"And risk getting Nore killed?" Jarman asked.

Baranov turned his eyes to the shark. "We can recapture his specimen. Divers can retrieve his computers from the wreckage. His data is secure. My country can supply scientists as well as geneticists from the Chinese government to duplicate his research."

Nore perked up. "Excuse me, Comrade?"

"Shut up, Nore," Baranov said.

"Nobody can duplicate my work. Only *I* understand the proper genetic sequencing to make the serum bond with the host's DNA."

"And that secret is locked in your computers. I'm aware they're sealed in secure cases inside the wreck," Baranov said.

Nore stepped forward as though to get in a physical altercation with the arms dealer, only to be held back by Weston. His jaw hung open, his mind searching for words. He was a man whose entire worldview had been shot down by a few words. His sense of importance, his confidence on his irreplaceability, the financial and personal security his work would provide—all of it imploded in the blink of an eye. Dr. Hank Nore was nothing more than a piece on a chess board. He had value, but in the eyes of the men with the funds, he was worth losing so long as he served his purpose.

"Damn," Jarman said. "So much for Nore having exceptional value. These guys are ready to gun him down right here."

"They'd rather have him dead than in the hands of our government," Serrano replied.

"Countdown starts now," Baranov announced. "Five…"

The revolver shook in a nervous Weston's grasp. "What's the call, boss? We going down in a blaze of glory?"

"Four…"

Jarman spat. "Certainly not selling my soul to these pricks."

"Three…

The crewmen steadied their assault rifles, ready to tear the American mercenaries apart.

"Just accept the offer," Nore said to Serrano. "Save yourself."

"You mean save you," Serrano replied.

"Two…"

Thud!

A tremor rippled underneath his boots again. The shark was still inspecting the vessel. Being half the size of the trawler, it was probably unsure if it wanted to commit to an attack.

"It's only a matter of time before it attacks," Nore said to Baranov.

"We have sedatives and towing cables. We'll have no problem getting the specimen to port." Baranov shifted his gaze to Serrano. "One…"

Serrano's index finger began to tighten on the pistol trigger. Zero was less than a second away. Thus, his life was about to conclude. If this was the end, he was going to go out with honor.

In the midst of this dark scenario came a tiny light. A literal light, shining from his wrist.

The watch had come back on. It was only at three percent power—enough to trigger a low-frequency soundwave.

He noticed a snarky grin on Jarman's face. On his belt was his smartphone. The light from its screen slipped through the edges of its case.

"Ta-da!"

Serrano smirked. The son of a bitch actually managed to get his phone to wirelessly charge the watch. As it turned out, Jarman could actually perform a little magic.

Serrano raised his hands, giving the illusion of surrendering to the opposition. It was enough to stall their gunfire long enough for him to slip the watch off. He pressed the low frequency button and tossed it over the port side of the boat. The sound coursed through the ocean, instantly driving the fish into a murderous frenzy.

First, Serrano heard the splash from its caudal fin slicing the water. Next, he saw the rolling waves in his peripheral vision and the torpedo shape moving toward the trawler's port quarter. Then came the impact.

The trawler rocked heavily to starboard, throwing everyone to their hands and knees. Up on the flying deck, Baranov was clinging to the guardrail, barely keeping himself from flinging over the side.

An echo of spiny flesh grinding against steel reverberated through the deck. The shark moved underneath the trawler, only to circle back and attack from the starboard side. Its snout punched the starboard bow, rocking the ship to port. Waves surged over the port bow as the fish pushed the vessel into a spin.

The deck was chaos. The Russian crew clearly did not understand what they were trying to recapture. In their minds, the shark was nothing more than a roided up fish. Capturing it would be no big deal.

Now, they were understanding the truth of what Dr. Nore had created.

Scattered on deck, the crewmen were caught between fending off the shark or gunning down the mercenaries. Three of them regained their balance and gathered on the starboard gunwale. Gunshots rang out, their bullets useless against the creature's thick hide.

Taking advantage of the chaos was Dr. Nore. The turbulence had loosened Weston's grip on his neck and shifted the position of his revolver, allowing the doctor to elbow him in the stomach. He followed it up by driving his heel into Weston's groin, effectively dropping the mercenary to his knees.

Nore sprinted up the deck, right past two rifle-bearing crewmen. Dedicated to their leader's instruction, they took aim at the mercenaries and squeezed the trigger.

BANG! BANG!

Both of them reeled backwards, their guns unleashing quick bursts of gunshots into the sky. They hit the deck, bleeding from bullet holes in their foreheads.

Serrano exhaled sharply, relieved to have been able to pull off accurate shots in the midst of extreme turbulence. The rest of the crew did not appear to notice the deaths of their comrades. The three on the starboard side were still shooting at the shark and the other two were attempting to climb a ladder to the wheelhouse, probably in hopes of driving the ship out of the area. As if the shark would not follow.

The spinning ceased, bringing a brief pause to the chaos. The shark disappeared under the waves, only to immediately reappear with open jaws. It breathed the water, arching its body over the starboard side. The three gunmen yelled out in terror.

The beast rose, raking the gunwale with its chin. One of the gunmen fell backward just in time. The other two were not so lucky.

With a mighty smack, the shark was back in the water. In its jaws were one of the gunmen, writhing in a world of agony.

The second gunman rolled with the waves, having been knocked overboard by the sweeping motion of its snout, but miraculously managing to avoid the clutches of its jaws. He emerged above the churning sea and took a breath, watching the shark seemingly bypass him.

Then came its tail.

SPLAT!

For those on deck, the splattering of his body was overtaken by the thud of the caudal fin striking the boat. Only when they saw the red droplets splashing above the gunnel did they realize the crewman had been smashed against the hull.

The shark traveled several meters behind the stern, leaving a trail of blood and guts in its wake. Once its jaws were finished with their work, it turned around and sped towards the trawler.

Serrano watched the fish dip a few meters under the surface. It moved in a vertical semi-circle, increasing speed with every passing moment. His throat tightened. The fish was about to breach again.

"Move! Move! Move!" he yelled. He grabbed Weston and threw him away from the transom. Jarman saw the danger for himself and came to the same conclusion Serrano had. He leapt from the transom right to the middle of the deck.

There was a wall of water, then the imploding of the transom. The shark's entire front half struck down on the vessel. The force of the impact tipped the trawler backward, turning its deck into a slope.

Caught on the edge, the shark's weight kept the vessel on an angle. Its red gums were entirely exposed. Fabric and soggy tissue dangled from its teeth. A horrid odor emitted from the back of its throat; the stench of death and digestion. It bit at the air, its body rocking side to side in an effort to slither up the deck like a snake and grab its next victim.

Serrano, Jarman, and Weston clawed at the deck, feeling gravity threatening to pull them into those snapping jaws. The Captain bent his fingers around the edge of a cargo hatch, keeping himself out of reach. A few feet to his right was Weston, who dug his fingertips into the deck textures. Serrano grabbed him by the arm and yanked him toward the hatch, giving him something more secure to hang on to.

Jarman was right below them. He had wedged his knife into the deck, essentially using it as an ice axe to prevent himself from sliding into the shark's mouth.

On the slope above them were the Russian crewmen. Two of them clung to the ladder, having failed in their attempt to reach the pilothouse. Dr. Nore was either on the foredeck or down below. Then there was the last gunman, who was in the process of sliding down the deck. He reached for anything they could, yelping with each passing inch.

He slipped past Serrano, yelling frantically as he came closer and closer to those jaws. That yelling amplified into a single high-pitched scream. It came straight from the back of the throat, demonstrating the pain and terror felt from teeth piercing his legs.

The shark remained in place, its mouth chomping away. Like a wheat grinder, it reduced its victim to pulp as gravity lowered him further into its jaws. The Russian disappeared into the back of its throat, his hands remaining outstretched the entire way.

"Oh, shit! Shit! CAPTAIN!"

Jarman was pointing at the flying bridge. Serrano lifted his gaze, just in time to see Baranov point his rifle at the mercenaries. In a swift motion, he extended his pistol and fired.

The bullet nicked Baranov's thigh, throwing his aim off right as he squeezed the trigger. His bullet zipped between Serrano and Weston, narrowly missing Jarman's temple before piercing the back of the shark's mouth.

As though hit by a bolt of lightning, the fish swung its body off the deck, freeing the boat from its weight.

The trawler leveled out, throwing the mercenaries forward. Serrano smacked face-down on the deck. When he looked up, he saw his pistol sliding from his grasp. It slid all the way to the base of the ladder. Above it was Baranov, still standing upright thanks to a tight grip on the guardrail.

The arms dealer took aim at the mercenaries and squeezed off a shot. One of the rounds punched through Weston's right shoulder, knocking him backward. Jarman grabbed ahold of him, preventing him from falling through the breach in the transom.

Serrano watched as that rifle muzzle pointed at him. Baranov cracked a smile, his way of letting the pesky gun-for-hire know he had gotten the better of him.

SPLASH!

Baranov turned to port, alarmed by the shark's reemergence. Its attention was not on the boat as a whole, but specifically on *him*. Only now did he understand the full magnitude of the project he was funding. The beast was not merely a wild animal, but a fiend with a lust for death. Unlike the normal members of its species, the shark held a grudge. Having taken a bullet in its mouth, it was eager to strike back.

"Come on, you bastard!" Baranov yelled. He hit the shark with several rounds. "I'm right here! Give me your best shot!"

It did.

Baranov grunted, feeling the penetrating force of a projectile thorn punching through his stomach. It struck with the force of a whaling harpoon, pinning him to the wheelhouse. He stared at its blunt end protruding from his midsection, then back at the shark. The life fled his body, rendering the expression of bewilderment permanent on his face.

Serrano hurried to Jarman and Weston.

"How's he doing?"

Weston groaned, sounding cranky rather than in pain. "I better get a raise."

Serrano chuckled. "Once we're out of this mess."

CRASH!!!

A tremendous impact rolled the boat to starboard.

"Speaking of which…" Jarman yanked Weston to his feet and pulled him to the portside. Their race to the gunwale quickly became an uphill one as the boat continued rolling to port. They barely managed to grab ahold of a cleat on the gunwale before the deck went vertical.

The trawler was on its side. Water consumed the main deck and pilothouse, flooding the interior. The last two Russian crewmen had finally reached the flying deck, only to be flung into the water. Churning waves carried them in opposite directions.

Serrano's luck didn't fare much better. Unable to grab ahold of anything, he was swept into the water. Large waves brushed him towards the bow. In his path was the trawler's mast, extending like an insect's antenna on a slight angle below the waves. Serrano grabbed ahold of the mast, preventing himself from being swept farther out.

He 'climbed' towards the ship's deck. All he could hope for at this point was to get inside and find an inflatable raft for he and his team.

A scream gave him pause. Looking to the east, he saw the shark raise its head. In its jaws was one of the Russian crewmen. Literally, his head and upper shoulders were in its mouth, his hands and feet flailing outside. Following a gut-wrenching crunching sound, the headless body fell free. The shark ignored the corpse in favor of the final crewman.

He swam feverishly out to sea, as though there was some sort of refuge out there on the horizon. It was a wasted effort. The shark slammed its jaws over his lower body and sharply turned east. Racing through the surface, it twisted into a corkscrew motion.

A stream of blood and limbs trailed behind it.

With nobody else in the water, Serrano knew he was next. He pulled himself to the flying bridge and grabbed ahold of the guardrail. There, he climbed to the wheelhouse door.

The shark resumed circling the boat in search of any other prey. The vessel remained in place, retaining its buoyancy despite taking on a significant amount of water.

"What's the plan, Captain?" Jarman shouted. He and Weston were resting on the portside hull overlooking the now-vertical deck.

Serrano ascended the guardrail and reached for the wheelhouse door.

"Kill the shark and find a way out of here."

His hand closed over the doorknob and twisted. The door fell open, revealing a crazed Dr. Nore clinging to the helm. He had a pistol in hand, aimed directly at Serrano.

"Not so fast, Captain!"

Serrano wasn't sure which was more bizarre: the existence of the mutated shark, or Dr. Nore's obsession with it.

"Jesus, Doctor! Are you for real? You're still trying to protect the damn thing?!"

"It is my creation!"

Had it been any other situation, Serrano would've thought Nore to be mimicking the mad scientists of old science-fiction movies. Yet, here he was, unironically declaring his devotion to the shark.

"Hate to break it to you, but it does not care," Serrano replied. "It doesn't see you as 'Daddy'. It sees you as a snack. To that thing, you're nothing more than a bag of potato chips."

The pistol shook in Nore's grasp. Blazing eyes burned into Serrano. No longer was the doctor calm, collected, and confident. All that was left was despair and anger.

"I created something nobody else ever could. You are just a soldier, Captain Serrano. People like you are a dime a dozen. You're replaceable. But me? Nobody can do what I do!"

Serrano shrugged. "Not according to Baranov."

"Baranov was a fool for believing his scientists could duplicate my work," Nore said. "Luckily for me, I know of a certain government who would gladly accept what I have to offer. Fortunately, it seems your objective is to take me to them *alive.*"

For a moment, a hint of Dr. Nore's usual confidence began to reemerge on his face.

Serrano could not help but laugh. Dr. Nore's half-smile instantly twisted into a look of bewilderment.

"Oh, Doctor. Tsk, tsk, tsk," Serrano said. "You might know a lot about genetics, but you're a shitty judge of character. You failed to see the obvious fact that Baranov thought you as nothing more than a tool. A tool that could easily be replaced by his own 'inferior' scientists." He watched Nore's face wrinkle with hatred. "Likewise, you've misjudged me. After what I've seen, frankly, I'm content with making sure your research dies here with you."

In the span of a few moments, Dr. Nore went through the five stages of grief. He smirked, thinking Serrano to be bluffing. When he realized the truth, that smirk turned into a demonic snarl, which then shifted into a wide-eyed expression of someone who had a new thought. In a split-second, he thought he could get Serrano to change his mind. The truth came over him like ash from a volcano, weighing his spirit down with a deep, dark reality. Everything he had worked for had amounted to nothing. His years of research, all of the ridicule from colleagues, the evasion of authorities, and deep plunge into treason—it all led to him being stranded out at sea.

In the end, he had no choice but to accept the reality of his fate. Inhaling deeply, he decided to compensate by outliving the mercenary who wrecked his plans.

He steadied his pistol and forced a grin.

"At least you'll die first. Should've followed the money instead of your integrity, you dumb son of a—"

For one final time, Nore's self-obsession had blinded him to the reality of his situation. Killing Serrano was not enough; he needed to get the last word in first.

In doing so, he never noticed the shark approaching the wheelhouse. Not until it punched through the windshield, that is.

Dr. Nore was swept up in a current of water and teeth. Like a bullet cutting through flesh, the shark's body ripped through the wheelhouse, shredding the interior, as well as its one occupant.

Its momentum took the fish directly towards Serrano. The mercenary released his grip on the guardrail and fell into the water. The ocean was quick to pull him out to sea, forcing him to grab ahold of the mast. He clung to its tip, watching in fascination as the shark burst from the rear of the wheelhouse. Clenched in its jaws was Dr. Nore. Retching his own blood, he reached out to Serrano as if there was any hope, or desire, for the mercenary to save him.

Gravity took hold of the fish, dropping it into the water, its flesh grazing the mast on which Serrano clung for dear life. It moved to the stern of the vessel, savoring the taste of its creator. Of course, the shark had no idea who Dr. Nore was.

As far as it was concerned, his only significance was tasting good.

It wasn't long before that dorsal fin angled to the left. The fish continued its roundabout until its snout was pointed right at Serrano.

He swallowed. "Oh, shit."

"Cap! It's coming back!" Jarman shouted.

"Oh, gee! Thanks! I couldn't tell!"

Like a torpedo cruising towards a battleship, the shark sped at the mercenary. Serrano hoisted himself onto the mast, planting his feet on the stem. He crouched and waited, watching the spiny bastard come at him.

Its jaws extended.

Serrano leapt. He cleared the snout and came down atop of the shark's head. The fish slammed its mouth shut, missing the human, instead biting the tip of the mast.

SNAP!

Spitting the severed wooden tip away, the shark swam out to sea with the human riding atop its head.

Serrano was on his knees, clinging to a pair of spines to prevent himself from being flung off. The shark reared its head back, sensing the intruder on top of it. Unable to snatch him off, it increased its speed and zigzagged across the water.

Serrano clung for dear life. Should the fish be successful in bucking him off, there would be nothing keeping it from tearing him apart.

The shark raised its upper body into the air and thrashed. Up, down, left, right—no amount of shaking could rid it of the pesky human. Frustrated, it submerged.

Serrano drew a breath and put all his energy into his grip. The shark raced underneath the trawler, veering sharply back and forth. Still feeling the mercenary clinging to its thorns, it went into a corkscrew spiral.

Serrano's entire body was parallel to the shark's, his feet whipping like kites. He gritted his teeth. His grasp on the thorns was starting to slip.

His troubles did not end there. He had only a couple of minutes left before he needed to breathe. It was not clear if the shark was intentionally utilizing that factor against him, but nonetheless, if he didn't break for the surface in the next couple of minutes, keeping away from its jaws would not make any difference. He would be equally as dead.

The shark stopped its spiral and moved in a straight line. It did not ascend. In fact, it appeared to be moving deeper.

Serrano felt his lungs starting to burn. The strain of the recent chaos had cost him of his air supply. The temptation to take his chances and swim for the surface began to eat at him. Serrano cursed in his mind. The rational part of his mind knew that was exactly what the shark wanted.

If only there was a way to distract it.

The shark turned left, causing his body to sway. Air bubbles shot from his mouth as Serrano yelped. A spine on the shark's neck had struck his leg.

The pain was the final straw for his psyche. It had been a long and exhausting day. Most of his men were dead, all thanks to this bastardization of nature. The stabbing of his leg was only the tip of the iceberg of misery.

All he could think of was payback.

Maintaining his grip on one of the spines, Serrano shifted to the right side of the creature's head. He leaned over until he was staring down at its large black eye. The big ball shifted slightly, glaring back at him.

Serrano drew his knife and raised it over his shoulder. There was another shift in the eyeball, followed by an acceleration of the shark's caudal fin. It *recognized* the weapon.

He brought the blade down with every ounce of force in his body. Snarling, he twisted the knife like the handle of a water pump, jettisoning a thick scarlet cloud.

The shark, half-blind and overloaded by pain, jerked back and forth. It moved left in a complete circle, then dove several meters.

Serrano twisted the knife again, triggering a new wave of pain.

In a lurching motion, the shark pointed its nose skyward. The tail moved side to side, propelling it at a forty-five-degree angle until it broke the surface like a rocket.

Serrano released the knife in favor of holding onto the spines. The shark hit the water with a tremendous splash, its tail still whipping about. It raced forward, half-blind.

To the right was the trawler.

Serrano gave another look at the knife, still embedded in the shark's eye socket. Strands of tissue clung to the serrated back edge, indicating it was fixed in there really well.

He grabbed the handle and pulled outward. The serrated edge racked the socket, sawing at the soft meat inside.

The shark lurched again. With the pain ripping through its head, it turned with the motion of the knife, putting itself on a collision course with the boat.

Serrano lowered his head and braced for impact.

Jarman and Weston, watching the events from atop the ship, simultaneously yelled "Holy shit!" before doing the same.

The shark smashed into the main deck. Its snout rammed through the deck, wedging itself into the cargo hold. It rocked its body and slashed its tail, frantically attempting to free itself.

"Hey, Cap!" Jarman shouted. "The hell are you doing riding a shark?"

Serrano looked up at him. "Glad you're amused! Mind helping me out?"

Weston leaned forward and extended his arm. In his hand was the snub nose .38 revolver.

"This is all we've got left, sir!" He tossed the weapon to the Captain.

Serrano held the revolver in front of his face, smirking at the irony of his situation.

Such a small gun to handle such a big shark. Then again…

"No such thing as too small a gun."

He leaned to the left, rammed the muzzle against the shark's other eye, and squeezed the trigger.

A marathon of rampaging motion followed. The shark was completely blind. It barrel rolled, tossing Serrano off its head. After a few rotations, it freed itself from the ship's deck and raced out to sea.

Serrano emerged and took a breath. For the third time, Serrano was clinging to the mast of the ship.

"There he is!" Jarman shouted. "He's alive."

"Cap! You alright?" Weston called out. "Where's the shark… Oh! Never mind!"

Serrano looked over his shoulder. There it was, writhing in a demonic fury a few yards behind him. The knife was still embedded in its head, angering the fish further.

"Oh damn, Cap!" Jarman shouted. "It looks pissed!"

"No shit, Jarman!"

Holding on to the mast of the ship, Serrano appraised the various courses of action he could take. He could join the others on the ship's hull and hope the shark went away. It was blind now, probably not focused on hunger.

Then again, hunger was not the soul motivation for its desire to kill. It was no longer a carnivorous animal who killed to survive. It was a cruel monster plagued with a desire to kill endlessly. Even without the use of its eyes, it would not leave until Serrano and his men were dead.

He had to kill it. The question was how. His knife and pistol were gone. The revolver had spent all of its rounds. All he had left were his fists and an empty gun. At this point, all he could do was hit it against the shark.

Serrano's eyes went to the tip of the mast. The shark had broken it when it went after him minutes ago, leaving a near-perfect point at the tip.

His mind went to the squid boat the shark had sunk that morning. The Captain had clung to the outrigger for dear life. The shark attacked, breaking the outrigger in half and nearly impaling itself in the process of killing the man.

It did not have the advantage of seeing the danger. All it could rely on were its hearing and sense of smell.

Serrano mounted the mast.

"Uh, boss?! What are you doing?" Jarman asked. "Get the hell out of the water!"

Serrano did not reply. Balancing his knees on the mast, he raised Weston's revolver and slammed it hard against the tip. The sound of impact traveled through the water.

He struck again. And again. And again.

The fish slowed its motions, detecting the low-frequency sounds echoing from the vessel. Its head, still bleeding from both eye sockets, turned to the source of the sound.

"Yeah, you hear that?" Serrano grumbled, watching the fish gradually increase speed. He struck the gun against the mast again. "You looking for me? I'm right over here."

The crescent-shaped tail whacked the ocean, jetting the angry beast to the familiar voice.

Serrano struck again.

"Come on! Take a big bite!"

He struck one last time.

The shark closed in. Its jaws extended to the max, revealing the back of its throat. A swipe of its tail accelerated it to a speed of fifty-miles-per-hour straight towards its adversary…

…and the trap he had in place.

Serrano jumped clear.

An explosion of crunching metal, splitting flesh, and spraying of blood echoed behind him. The shark, skewered on the mast, shook its body. The tip had run through its mouth all the way through its stomach. Rivers of blood streamed from its mouth, gills, and eye sockets.

Serrano surfaced and looked upon his work.

The titan prototype was impaled on the mast, its desire to kill having led to its own demise.

"Chew on that."

CHAPTER 13

"Well hot damn, Captain!" Jarman said. "You never cease to amaze me!"

Serrano emerged from the trawler's wheelhouse. After killing the shark, he began searching the vessel for any inflatable life rafts and any other equipment they could use. The results did not disappoint.

A pull of a ripcord inflated a large red raft.

Jarman and Weston moved to the bow of the ship where it was easier to board the inflatable. Serrano lifted a few emergency kits onto the raft, then pulled himself aboard.

"How's the wound?" he asked.

"Hurts," Weston said, groaning. "But I'll live."

Serrano tossed him his revolver. "Here's your gun back. Sorry if it's a little dinged."

Weston chuckled. "That's alright. I can take it to a shop and get it fixed up."

"It's a great gift," Serrano said. He tapped Weston on his good shoulder. "Your son chose well."

Jarman ruffled through the supplies. "Got some food, a flare pistol, some medical supplies… Oh, look at this!" He held up a satellite phone.

"Yeah, found that in the wheelhouse," Serrano said.

"Who we gonna call first?" Weston asked. Immediately, Jarman snorted and covered his face, unsure whether to make the obvious joke. Weston pointed a finger. "If you say *Ghostbusters*, I'm gonna have the Captain throw your ass overboard."

Serrano took the phone. "I'll get ahold of one of our associates and have them get a response team out here."

"Not gonna call the government?" Jarman asked.

Serrano turned his eyes to the dead shark and shook his head.

"Nope. As long as I can help it, nobody's getting their hands on this thing's DNA. Dr. Nore's research dies today."

Weston nodded in agreement. "No arguments here."

Jarman nodded, though with less enthusiasm. Not having Dr. Nore and the specimen likely meant a smaller payday. However, he knew destroying the creature was the right thing to do. Not all things were worth the money.

"I guess we'll be floating out here for a while," he said.

"Yep." Serrano began tending to Weston's injury. "We've got a lot of time to kill. Hope you guys have some ideas on how to kill the boredom."

Jarman perked up. "I could show you some new magic tricks."

Both Serrano and Weston looked at him. At once, they replied, "No, thanks. We're good."

They shared a laugh and began the long wait for rescue.

@severedpress
/severedpress

Check out other great

Sea Monster Novels!

Michael Cole

SCAR

Scar is a killing machine. Born from DNA spliced between the extinct Megalodon and modern day Great White, he has a viciousness that transcends time. His evil is reflected in his eyes, his savagery in his two-inch serrated teeth, his ruthlessness in his trail of death. After escaping captivity, the killer shark travels to the island community Cross Point, where prey is in abundance. With an insatiable appetite, heightened senses, and skin impervious to bullets, Scar kills everything that crosses his path. His reign of terror puts him at war with the island sheriff, Nick Piatt. With the body count rising, Nick vows to protect his island community from the vicious threat. With the aid of a marine biologist, a rookie deputy, and a bad-tempered fisherman, Nick leads a crusade against Scar, as well as the ruthless scientist who created him.

Rick Chesler

HOTEL MEGALODON

An underwater luxury hotel on a gorgeous tropical island is set for an extravagant opening weekend with the world watching. The only thing standing in the way of a first-rate experience for the jet-setting VIPs is an unscrupulous businessman and sixty feet of prehistoric shark. As the underwater complex is besieged by a marauding behemoth, newly minted marine biologist Coco Keahi must face off against the ancient predator as it rises from the deep with a vengeance. Meanwhile, a human monster has decided he would be better off if Coco were one of the creature's victims.

www.ingramcontent.com/pod-product-compliance
Lightning Source LLC
Chambersburg PA
CBHW061240170626
46809CB00007B/2764

* 9 7 8 1 9 2 3 1 6 5 8 9 2 *